Fanchon the Cricket

or

"La Petite Fadette"

MADAME DUDEVANT.—1804-1876.

"George Sand" is acknowledged to be the greatest of women novelists, and the master of French prose writers. She is best known to the English public by her series of pastorals, or stories of village life (like *Fanchon*), and by these she will be longest remembered. *Fanchon* was dramatized and played all over the world. With the inward eye she sees into the life of things; she seizes with her pencil the visionary gleam; she shows the mystical influences which emanate from the world of sense, the witchery of the sky, the quiet soul of the river, the beauty born of murmuring sound, the grey *landes* stretching far away to the blue horizon, the deep-meadowed champaigns with orchard lawns and bowery hollows.

Fanchon the Cricket

or

"La Petite Fadette"

by

GEORGE SAND

With a New Chronology of Her Life and Work

CASSANDRA EDITIONS
An Imprint Of
ACADEMY PRESS LIMITED
Chicago
1977

Cassandra Editions 1977
Chronology © Academy Press Limited 1977

All rights reserved by
Academy Press Limited
360 North Michigan Avenue, Chicago, Illinois 60601

Printed and Bound in the United States of America

Sand, George, pseud. of Mme. Dudevant, 1804-1876.
  Fanchon, the cricket; or, La petite Fadette.

  Reprint of the 1871 ed. published by T.B. Peterson,
Philadelphia.
  I. Title.
PZ3.S21Fan   1977   [PQ2411.P4]   843'.8   77-14025
ISBN 0-915864-36-3 pbk.
ISBN 0-915864-37-1 lib. bdg.

This edition published with the cooperation
of the Hamilton, Ontario, Canada, public library.

GEORGE SAND: CHRONOLOGY

1804
July 1 Birth at 15 Rue de la Meslay, Paris. Daughter of
Maurice Dupin and Sophie Delaborde. Christened Amandine
Aurore Lucie Dupin.
Family moves to Rue de la Grange-Batelière, Paris.

1808
Aurore travels to Spain with her mother. They join her father
at Palace de Goday in Madrid, where he is serving in Napoleon's army under General Murat.

1809
The family goes to Nohant in France, the home of Maurice
Dupin's mother, born Marie-Aurore de Saxe, Comtesse de
Horn, the daughter of the illegitimate son of King Frederic-
Augustus II of Poland. Death of Maurice Dupin in a fall from
a horse.

1810
Sophie Dupin gives custody of Aurore to Madame Dupin in
return for a pension.

1810-1814
Winters in Paris at Rue Neuve-des-Mathurins with her
grandmother and visits from Sophie. Summers at Nohant.

1817-1820
Educated at the English Convent des Augustines in Paris.

1820
Returns to Nohant. Studies with her father's tutor Deschar-
tres.

1821
Death of Madame Dupin. Aurore inherits some money, a house in Paris and the house at Nohant.
Moves in with her mother at 80 Rue St.-Lazare, Paris.

1822
Meets Casimir Dudevant on a visit to the Duplessis family.
September 10 Marries Dudevant, son of Baron Dudevant.
They move to Nohant.

1823
June 30 Maurice is born at Hotel de Florence, 56 Rue Neuve-des-Mathurins, Paris.

1824
Spring and summer at the Duplessis' at Plessis-Picard near Melun; autumn at a Parisian suburb, Ormesson; winter in an apartment at Rue du Faubourg-Saint-Honoré.

1825
Spring at Nohant. Aurore is ill in the summer. Dudevants travel to his family home in Gascony. She meets Aurélian de Sèze, and recovers her health.
November 5 Writes long confession to Casimir about de Sèze. She gives him up.
Winter in Gascony.

1826
Moves to Nohant. Casimir travels, Aurore manages the estate and writes to de Sèze.

1827
Illness again. The water cure at Clermont-Ferraud, where she writes *Voyage En Auvergne,* autobiographical sketch.

1827-1829
Winter at Le Châtre. Summer at Nohant.

1828
September 13 Birth of Solange.

1830
Visit to Bordeaux to Aurélian de Sèze. Their correspondence ceases. She writes a novel *Aimée*.
December Discovery of Casimir's will, filled with antipathy to her.

1831
January 4 Moves to Paris to 31 Rue de Seine.
Joins staff of *Le Figaro*. Writes three short stories: *La Molinara* (in *Figaro*); *La Prima Donna* (in *Revue de Paris)* and *La Fille d'Albano* (in *La Mode*).
April Returns to Nohant for three months. Writes *Indiana*.
July Moves to 25 Quai Saint-Michel, Paris.
December Publishes *Rose Et Blanche* in collaboration with Jules Sandeau. Book is signed Jules Sand.

1832
Travel between Paris and Nohant.
April Solange is brought to Paris.
November Move to 19 Quai Malaquais with Solange.
Indiana and *Valentine* published. Maurice sent by Casimir to Henry IV Military Academy in Paris.

1833
January Break with Sandeau.
June Meets Alfred de Musset.
Publishes *Lelia*.
September Fontainebleau with de Musset.
December 12 To Italy with de Musset.

1834

January 19 The Hotel Danieli in Venice. Musset attempts a break with Aurore, becomes ill. His physician is Pietro Pagello.

March 29 de Musset returns to Paris. Aurore remains with Pagello.

Writes *André, Mattéa, Jacques, Léone Léoni* and the first *Lettres d'Un Voyageur*.

August 15 Return to Paris with Pagello.

August 24 de Musset goes to Baden.

August 29 Aurore to Nohant.

October Return to Paris. Musset return from Baden. Pagello returns to Venice.

November 25 Begins journal to de Musset.

December Return to Nohant.

1835

January Return to Paris.

March 6 Final break with Musset.

Meets Michel of Bourges, her lawyer and political mentor.

Writes *Simon.*

Autumn Return to Nohant for Maurice's holiday.

October 19 Casimir threatens her physically. Begins suit for legal separation.

December 1 Judgment in her favor won by default.

1836

February 16 She wins second judgment. Casimir bring suit.

May 10, 11 Another verdict in her favor from civil court of La Châtre. Casimir appeals to a higher court.

July 25, 26 Trial in royal court of Bourges. Jury divided. Out of court settlement. Her fortune is divided with Casimir.

August To Switzerland with Maurice and Solange and Liszt and d'Agoult.

Autumn Hotel de la France, 15 Rue Lafitte, Paris with Liszt and d'Agoult. Meets Chopin.

1837

January Return to Nohant. Publishes *Mauprat* in spring. Writes *Les Maîtres Mosaïstes*. Liszt and d'Agoult visit Nohant. Fatal illness of Sophie in Paris. Visit to Fontainebleau, writes *La Dernière Aldini*. Trip to Gascony to recover Solange, who has been kidnapped by Casimir.

1838

Writes *L'Orco* and *L'Uscoque,* two Venetian novels.
May To Paris. Romance with Chopin.
November Trip to Majorca with children and Chopin. Writes *Spiridion.*

1839

February Leaves Majorca for three months in Marseilles. Then to Nohant. Publishes *Un Hiver À Majorque, Pauline* and *Gabriel-Gabrielle.*
October Occupies adjoining apartments with Chopin until spring of 1841 at 16 Rue Pigalle, Paris, in winter. Summer is spent at Nohant with Chopin as guest.

1840

Writes *Compagnon Du Tour De France* and *Horace.* Influenced by Pierre Leroux.

1841

Moves from Rue Pigalle to 5 and 9 Rue St.-Lazare, Square d'Orléans, with Chopin.

1842

Consuelo published.

1843

La Comtesse De Rudolstadt published, a sequel to *Consuelo.*

1844

Jeanne published, a foreshadowing of pastoral novels.

1845
Tévérino, Péché de M. Antoine and *Le Meunier D'Angibault,* the latter two socialist novels.

1846
La Mare Au Diable published and *Lucrezia Floriani.* Solange married to Auguste-Jean Clésinger. Estrangement from Chopin.

1847
François Le Champi published.

1848
Writes government circulars, contributes to *Bulletins de la Republique* and publishes her own newspaper *La Cause du Peuple,* all for the Second Republic. Death of Solange's son. *La Petite Fadette* published.

1849
Her play based on *François Le Champi* performed at the Odéon. First of a series of successful plays.

1850
Chateau des Désertes published in the *Revue Des Deux Mondes.*

1851
Republic falls. She uses her influence to save her friends from political reprisals. Plays *Claudie* and *Le Mariage De Victorine* presented.

1852
Return to Nohant.

1853
Published *Les Maitres Sonneurs.* Play *Le Pressoir* presented.

1855
Four volume autobiography *Histoire De Ma Vie* published, carries her life to Revolution of 1848.
January 13 Death of Solange's daughter Jeanne.
Visit to Italy with Maurice and Alexandre Manceau.

1856
Does French adaptation of *As You Like It*.

1858
Holidays at Gargilesse on River Creuse at cottage given her by Alexander Manceau.

1859
Writes *Elle Et Lui*. Publishes *Jean De La Roche* and *L'Homme De Neige*.

1860
Writes *La Ville Noire* and *Marquis De Villemer*.
November Contracts typhoid fever.

1862
May 16 Marriage of Maurice Sand and Caroline Calametta.

1863
July 14 Marc-Antoine Sand born, son of Maurice and Caroline.
Mademoiselle La Quintinie published, anti-clerical novel.
Begins friendship with Flaubert.

1864
Play *Le Marquis De Villemer* presented. Death of Marc-Antoine Sand. Moves from 3 Rue Racine near the Odéon to 97 Rue des Feuillantines. Exchanges Gargilesse for a house at Palaiseau with Manceau.

1865
Death of Manceau.

1866
Visits Flaubert at Croisset, dedicates *Le Dernier Amour* to him. Birth of Aurore Sand.

1867
Return to Nohant to live with Maurice and Caroline. Writes two novels a year.

1868
Birth of Gabrielle Sand.

1870
The play *L'Autre* with Sarah Bernhardt, presented at the Theatre Français.

1870-1871
Franco-German War. Removal to Boussac because of a small-pox epidemic at Nohant.

1876
June 8 Dies.

FANCHON THE CRICKET

CHAPTER I.

FARMER BARBEAU, of La Cosse, was in comfortable circumstances, as was evidenced by his being a member of the municipal council of his commune. He was the owner of two fields, which, besides affording support to his family, brought him considerable profit, for they yielded abundant crops of hay which was prized as the best fodder in the neighborhood.

Barbeau's house was well built, roofed with tiles, and stood in a fine position on the side of a hill, with an excellent garden and vineyard attached. At the rear of his barn he had a capital orchard, producing an abundance of plums, cherries, apples, pears, while his walnut trees were the largest and oldest within six miles of the spot. He was a kind-hearted and industrious man, strongly attached to his family, without being unjust to his neighbors and fellow-parishioners.

He already had three children, when mother Barbeau, doubtless taking into consideration that they had sufficient means for five, and no time to lose, thought fit to give him at a birth two fine

boys, so much alike that it was almost impossible
to distinguish one from the other.

Dame Sagette, who received them in her apron
as they came into the world, did not omit to make
a little cross with her needle upon the arm of the
firstborn; "for," said she, "a ribbon, or a neck-
lace may easily get changed, and then the right of
primogeniture will be lost to the eldest, and as
soon as the child is strong enough," she added,
"you must make a mark which can never be ef-
faced." A piece of advice which was not forgotten.

The eldest was christened Sylvain, which name
was converted into Sylvinet, to distinguish him
from his eldest brother, who had stood as god-
father to him; while the younger was called Landry, a name which he preserved as he had received
it at his baptism, since his uncle, who was his god-
father, had, from his youth upward, been called
Landriche.

Farmer Barbeau was somewhat astonished
when he returned from market to see two little
heads in the cradle. "Oh! oh!" said he, "this
cradle is too small. To-morrow I must make it
larger."

Though he had never learned it as a trade, he
knew something of joining, and had made more
than half of his own furniture. The worthy man
gave no further evidence of surprise, but went to
see his wife, who drank a large glass of warm
wine and declared that she never was better in her
life.

"You do so much, wife," he said to her, "that I must take fresh courage. Here are two more children to provide for, whom we did not absolutely need, and this is a hint to me that I must not flag in the culture of my lands and cattle. But be easy; they, too, will work bye and bye; and take care you do not give me three next time, for that would be rather too much." At this Mother Barbeau began to shed tears, which greatly distressed her good man.

"Come, come," said he, "you must not grieve, wife. It was not to reproach you I spoke thus, but on the contrary to thank you. These two children are fine, well-made little fellows, sound in body and limb, and I am grateful."

"Alas!" said the wife, "I know well you did not mean to reproach me; but I am sadly troubled, for they tell me there is nothing more difficult to rear than twins; that they wrong each other, and that frequently one of the two must perish that its twin may thrive."

"Indeed," said the farmer, "is that true? As for me, these are the first twins I have seen. It is not a common event. But here is dame Sagette, who knows something about these things, and who will tell us all about it."

Dame Sagette being thus called upon, replied: "You may rely upon what I tell you; your twins will both thrive. I have exercised my profession for half a century, and during that time I have seen all the children of the district born; these, therefore. are not the first twins I have brought

into the world. Now the resemblance does not
affect their health at all; there are twins who are
no more like each other than you and I; but it
often happens that one is strong and the other
weak, and that is why one lives and the other dies.
But look at yours; they are both as strong and
healthy as though they were only sons. They are
beautiful children, and there is no fear of their
dying. Console yourself, therefore, mother Barbeau; it will be a pleasure to you to watch them
grow, and if they continue as they have begun, it
will be only you and those who see them every
day who will be able to distinguish between them,
for I never saw twins so much alike. They re-
semble newly-hatched partridges; none but the
mother-bird can tell one from the other."

"This is all very well," said Barbeau, scratching
his head; "but I have heard it said that twins take
such an affection for one another that when they
are separated they refuse to live, and that one is
often so consumed with grief as to perish."

"And that is true," returned Dame Sagette.
"But listen to what a woman of experience is
about to tell you, and be sure you do not forget;
for when your children are old enough to be separated, I shall, perhaps, be no longer in the world
to counsel and advise you. Take care, as soon as
your twins begin to know each other, that you do
not allow them to be always together. Set one to
work, while the other remains in the house.
When one goes fishing send the other hunting;
when one looks after the sheep let the other attend

to the oxen; when you give one wine to drink let the other have water. Do not scold or correct them at the same time; do not dress them alike; when one has a hat let the other have a cap; and, above all, do not let their blouses be of the same color. In short, by all means you can devise, prevent them from being accustomed to be taken for each other. I fear greatly that what I am now telling you will go in at one ear and out of the other; but if you do not attend to it you will some day bitterly repent."

Dame Sagette spoke golden words. They promised to do as she directed, and dismissed her with a present. Then, as she had strongly recommended that the twins should not be nourished with the same milk, they set about inquiring for a wet-nurse; but there was none to be found in the neighborhood. Mother Barbeau, who had not made her calculations for twins, and who had herself nursed the rest of the children, was, of course, unprepared for such an emergency. The farmer was therefore obliged to set out in quest of a nurse; and during this interval, as the mother could not allow her little ones to suffer, she gave the breast to both infants alike. The matter of engaging a nurse was not pressing, for two such young children could not distress their mother, and they were so healthy, so quiet and good, that the two scarcely caused more disturbance in the house than one. When one slept the other slept also. The father had altered the cradle, so that when the twins cried, as they always did at the same

time, they were cradled and rocked together. At
last, when Farmer Barbeau had arranged with a
nurse, his wife said to him:

"Husband, I do not see why we should spend
so much money, as if we were gentlemen and
ladies, or as if I were too old to nurse my children,
when I have more milk than they want. Our
boys are already a month old, and see what splen-
did condition they are in. The woman whom
you would give to one of them as nurse is not half
so strong and healthy as myself; her milk is older,
and not what so young a child requires. It is true
La Sagette told us not to nourish our twins with
the same milk, to prevent them imbibing too
strong an affection for each other, but did she not
also tell us that we must take equal care of both,
since twins are not so strong as other children?
Now, I would rather that ours should love each
other too much than that either should be sacri-
ficed. Moreover, which of the two should we put
out to nurse? I confess I should be as grieved to
part with one as with the other, for though I can
say honestly that I have always loved my children
dearly, these two seem to me the dearest and prettiest I have ever borne in my arms. I beg of you,
therefore, to think no more of this nurse; for the
rest, we will do all La Sagette recommended."

"What you say seems reasonable," replied Barbeau, looking at his wife; "but suppose that in
proportion as these children grow your health
should decline?"

"Do not fear," said she; "I have as good an

appetite as though I were only fifteen, and besides, if I should feel my strength giving way, I promise you not to conceal it, and it will then be time enough to send one of these poor babes away."

Upon this Barbeau gave up the point, all the more readily that he did not care to incur the unnecessary expense. Mother Barbeau nursed her twins without either suffering or complaint, and two years after her little ones were weaned, she gave birth to a pretty little girl, who was christened Nanette, and whom also she nursed.

Thus the family grew and played together in the sunshine, none noisier or better behaved than the rest.

CHAPTER II.

THE twins grew without experiencing more illness than falls to the lot of most children; they were even gifted with such sweet and gentle dispositions that they might be said to suffer less with their teeth and the maladies incidental to childhood than the rest of the little world.

They were fine, fair children, with large blue eyes, broad shoulders, straight, well-poised figures, possessing greater strength than others of their age, so that passers-by would stop to look at them, exclaiming: "They are indeed a couple of handsome lads."

Thus, accustomed from an early age to be no-

ticed and questioned, the twins escaped the stupid
bashfulness of adolescence, and were at their ease
with every one. Instead of hiding themselves
among the bushes, they would meet a stranger
frankly, and would reply to all that was asked
without hanging their heads or waiting to be en-
treated. At the first glance there was no percep-
tible difference between them; they were as like
as two eggs; but a quarter of an hour's observation would show that Landry was a trifle the taller
and stronger, that his hair was somewhat thicker,
his nose larger, and his eyes more brilliant. He
had also a broader forehead and a more decided
air, and a mark which his brother had on the right
cheek was more plainly visible on his left. Their
neighbors could therefore distinguish them well
enough, though it took even them a second to
decide; but after dark, or at a little distance, all
were liable to be mistaken, inasmuch as the voices
of the twins were alike, and, knowing that they
might be mistaken for one another, they were
accustomed to answer at random, without giving
themselves the trouble to point out a mistake.
Even Barbeau himself was sometimes at a loss.
Thus, as La Sagette had predicted, it was the
mother only who was never mistaken, whether at
night, or at such a distance that she could but just
see or hear them speak. In short, one was the
counterpart of the other; and if Landry were a
trifle more courageous and gay, Sylvinet was so
affectionate and intelligent that it was impossible
to love him less. For three months both father

and mother had entertained the idea of preventing the twins from forming too strong an attachment, and three months is a long time for country people to observe anything contrary to custom. Then, on the one side, they did not see that any great effect was produced, and, by degrees, the worthy pair forgot all they had promised to perform. Thus, when frocks were exchanged for breeches, not only did a petticoat of the mother serve for the two garments, but the fashion was exactly the same, the tailor of the parish not being skilled in any other. As the twins grew up, a similarity of taste in color manifested itself, and when their aunt Rosette wished to present them with a cravat for a New Year's present, they both chose the same lilac neckerchief from the stores of the pedler, who trafficked from door to door on the back of a horse. Their aunt inquired if this choice arose from any fancy of being always dressed alike; to which Sylvinet replied that it was the prettiest cravat both in color and design, and Landry immediately assured her that all the rest were villainous.

"And the color of my horse," said the peddler, smiling, "what do you think of that?"

"It is very ugly," said Landry; "it is like an old magpie."

"It is ugly, indeed," reiterated Sylvinet, "and is exactly like a magpie with faded plumage."

"You perceive," said the peddler to the aunt, with a shrewd look, "these children see with the same eyes. Were one to see yellow red, the other

would immediately see red yellow; and they must
not be thwarted or opposed; for it is said, that
when people try to prevent twins from looking on
themselves as prints of the same design, they become idiots, and no longer know what they say."

The mercer said this because the lilac cravats
were of a bad tint, and he desired to get rid of
them.

Thenceforth, everything went on in the same
way, and the twins were dressed so exactly alike
that they were oftener than ever mistaken for each
other. Either from childish mischief, or by reason of that law of nature which some believe it
impossible to set aside, when one broke the toe of
his sabot, the other would immediately chip his on
the same foot, and when one tore his jacket or cap,
the other, without loss of time, would imitate the
rent so well, that it would be supposed the same
accident had befallen both; and when asked how
the misfortune had happened, the twins would
laugh, or put on an air of surprise and innocence.

For good or ill, this friendship grew with their
growth, till the day arrived when these twins declared that they could not play with other children
if either were absent; and the farmer trying, on
a certain occasion, to keep one with him while the
other remained with the mother, both became so
sad, pale, and listless, that it was feared they would
be ill; and when at length the evening arrived,
and with it their reunion, they rambled away,
hand in hand, refusing to return home, so glad
were they to be together again, and so vexed

that their parents had caused them this sorrow. They were never again subjected to this trial, for it must be confessed that father and mother, uncles and aunts, brothers and sisters, all entertained for the twins an affection amounting almost to weakness. They were proud of them, not only for the compliments they were constantly receiving on their account, but because they were a pair of handsome, well-disposed boys. From time to time Barbeau grew somewhat uneasy as to the result of their being so constantly together, and, recalling the words of La Sagette, tried to provoke them into jealousy of each other. Thus, when they had committed some trifling fault, he would pull the ears of Sylvinet, saying to Landry: "For this once I forgive you, because you are usually the most reasonable."

But it consoled Sylvinet for the tingling of his own ears to see that his brother was spared, while Landry wept as though he had received the correction. At other times, Barbeau would give to one only what both greatly desired; but, if it were something to eat, they immediately shared it between them; or, if it were a plaything, they would use it in common, or give and retake it without distinction of *meum* and *tuum*. If one were praised at the expense of the other, the other was proud and happy to see his twin encouraged, and would praise him also. In short, it was labor thrown away to try and divide them in mind or body, and, as it is not pleasant to oppose those

whom we love, matters were soon allowed to take
their course.

The boys were full of mischief, and that they
might be left in peace, would sometimes pretend
to quarrel and dispute; but, if any idler evinced
surprise, they would run away and conceal themselves, to laugh at his expense, and would be
heard chattering and singing together like a
couple of blackbirds among the bushes.

Notwithstanding the strong resemblance and
the great attachment which existed between
them, God, who makes no two things absolutely
alike, either in heaven or earth, decreed that their
fate should be very different.

The proof of all things lies in trial, and, in this
instance, the trial took place subsequent to the
first communion of the twins. Farmer Barbeau's
family, thanks to his two elder daughters, was
constantly on the increase. His eldest son, Sylvain, a fine young fellow, was at service; his sons-
in-law were industrious, but work was not always
to be had. A succession of bad years, caused by
the inclemency of the seasons and commercial
pressure, had taken more crowns from the pockets
of the farmers than had been put into them, so
that Father Barbeau, not being rich enough to
keep all his family with him, was obliged to think
of sending his twins from home. Farmer Caillaud offered to take one as herdsman, as he had a
large farm to cultivate, and his own boys were
either too old or too young for such work.
Mother Barbeau, when her husband first broke

the subject, was greatly grieved; to all appearances such a thought had never entered her head, though, in reality, it had haunted her from the hour of their birth; but, as in all things she was accustomed to yield to her husband, she knew not what to urge against the proposal. Barbeau himself was considerably perplexed, and gently prepared the way with his twins. At first they wept bitterly, and passed three whole days wandering about the woods and meadows, returning only to their meals. Not a word did they say to their parents, and when asked if they had determined upon submitting to necessity, instead of replying, held fresh converse together.

The first day they could do nothing but lament, clasping each other by the arm as though they feared to be separated by force. But Barbeau never thought of resorting to such means. He was strong in the wisdom of the peasant, which consists half in patience, and half in reliance on the effect of time. Thus, on the morrow, finding they were not interfered with, and that their parents relied on their good sense, the twins grew more amenable to the paternal will than the severest measures could have rendered them.

"We shall be obliged to yield," said Landry; "it remains only to decide which of us shall go, for they have left the choice to ourselves, and Farmer Caillaud says he cannot take both."

"What does it matter to me whether I go or remain," returned Sylvinet, "since we are forced to part? I do not care for being elsewhere; if we could only be together I should soon get reconciled to another home."

"That may be," said Landry; "yet the one who remains here will suffer less than he who has to leave brother, father, mother, garden, cattle, everything in which he has been accustomed to take pleasure."

Landry said this in a firm tone, but Sylvinet began weeping afresh, for he lacked the resolution of his brother, and the bare idea of losing all at the same time caused him such pain that he could no longer restrain his tears. Landry wept also, but less vehemently, and from a different cause. He had resolved to take the heavier sorrow upon himself, and only desired to see how much his brother could bear, that he might spare him the rest. He knew well that Sylvinet was more alarmed than himself at the thought of going to a strange place, and living with any other family than his own.

"Come, brother," said he, "if we can but determine to part, it is better that I should go. I am somewhat the stronger, and when we are ill the fever runs higher with you than with me. They say we may perhaps die if we are parted; I do not think I shall, but I would not answer for you, and this is why I would rather you should remain with our mother, who will know how to comfort and console you. Moreover, if there be any difference between us, I think you are the favorite, and I know you are the most delicate and sensitive. Do you then remain and let me go. We shall not be far from each other; the grounds of Farmer Caillaud join ours, and we can meet every day. I like work, and it will serve to amuse me. Then, I run faster than you, and can join you all the more quickly as soon as I have finished my day's labor. Indeed, I shall be far happier than if you were away and I at home; so stay, I entreat you."

CHAPTER III.

SYLVINET would not listen to this proposal. Though it was true that he entertained a more tender affection for his father and mother, and his little sister Nanette, than did Landry, yet he shrunk from laying the whole burden upon his beloved twin.

After much discussion, they at last determined to draw lots, and the lot fell to Landry. Sylvinet was not satisfied with this trial, and insisted upon tossing up with a penny. Three times the copper fell in his favor; it was ordained that Landry should go.

"You see fate will have it so," said Landry, "and you know we must not oppose fate."

The third day arrived; Sylvinet still wept bitterly, but Landry scarcely cried at all. The first idea of leaving home had perhaps caused him more pain than his brother, since he had at once felt his own strength, and the uselessness of resisting his parents' wishes; thus, by boldly con-

2

fronting his sorrow, he had disarmed it of its
sting, and had been able to reason coolly and
calmly with himself; while Sylvinet, yielding to
his grief, had not found courage to reason at all;
so that Landry had resolved to depart, while Sylvinet was still unprepared to let him go.

Landry had more self-respect than his brother.
The twins had so often been told that they would
never be men unless they accustomed themselves
to live apart, that Landry, with the pride natural
to his fourteen years, had a great desire to show
he was no·longer a child.   From their first birds-
nesting to the present moment, he had always
been the one to counsel and direct his brother; he
succeeded now in soothing him; and at evening,
upon their return to the house, he announced to
his father that his brother and he were prepared
to submit to their duty; that they had drawn lots;
and that it was for him, Landry, to go as herdsman.

Upon this, Barbeau, though they were already
stout lads, took one of his twins upon each knee,
and thus addressed them: "My children, I see,
by your submission, that you have arrived at years
of discretion, and I am thankful for it.   Remember that when children do the will of their parents
they also do that of the great God of Heaven, who
will some day reward them for it.   I do not desire
to know which of you was the first to submit, God
knows, and He will bless that one for having
spoken wisely, as He will bless the other for having listened."   Having said this, he conducted

the twins to their mother, that they might also receive her approval, but Mother Barbeau found it so difficult to restrain her tears that she could say nothing, and contented herself with embracing them in silence.

Barbeau knew very well which of the two was the most courageous and affectionate. He resolved not to allow time for Sylvinet's good resolutions to cool, for he saw that Landry was decided, and that the grief of his brother could alone shake his resolution. He therefore roused Landry before daybreak, taking good care not to disturb Sylvinet, who slept by his side.

"Come, my boy," said he in a whisper, "we must set out before your mother sees you, for you know how grieved she is to part with you, and we must spare her all we can. I will accompany you to your new master's, and will carry your bundle."

"Shall I not say good-bye to my brother?" asked Landry. "He will be vexed if I leave him without saying a word."

"Should your brother awake and find you departing, he would cry, and that would arouse your mother, and your mother would grieve all the more for the sorrow of her children. Come, Landry, you are a fine spirited boy, and would not willingly make your mother ill. Go through with your duty, my child, and depart without making a scene. This evening I will bring your brother to see you, and, as to-morrow is Sunday, you will come and spend the day with your mother."

Landry obeyed bravely, and passed through the
door of the house without looking behind him.
His mother, however, was not so fast asleep or so
tranquil in her mind but that she heard all which
passed between her good man and Landry. But
the poor woman, feeling the reasonableness of
what he said, did not move, and contented herself
with drawing her curtain aside, that she might see
Landry go out; then her heart was so full that she
jumped out of bed to follow and embrace him, but
the bed of the twins, where Sylvinet still soundly
slept, stopped her. The poor lad had cried for
three days and three nights, and was overcome by
fatigue, and feverish and restless, turned and
tossed upon his mattress, uttering moans and
sighs in his sleep.

Mother Barbeau, gazing upon the only twin
left to her, could not help feeling that this was the
one whose absence would have grieved her the
most. Beyond doubt, Sylvinet was the most affectionate of the two; whether it were from a more
sensitive organization, or that God, in his law of
nature, decrees that where two persons love each
other, either as friends or lovers, one must ever
give more of his heart than the other. Now, Barbeau's preference was for Landry, inasmuch as he
valued industry and courage more than affection
and gentleness, while the mother's, as has been
shown, was for the loving and tender-hearted Sylvinet.

Thus, as she stood gazing on her poor boy, so
pale and haggard, she could not help saying to

herself, that it was a pity to bring him to such a
condition; that her Landry was better fitted to
encounter hardships, and that affection for his
twin and mother would never endanger his life.

"The boy has a great sense of duty," thought
she, "but, if he were not a little hard-hearted he
could not have departed like that, without a mur-
mur, without looking behind him, or shedding a
single tear. He would not have found strength
to go without asking courage of the good God,
and he would have come to my bed, where I lay
pretending to sleep, had it been only to take a last
look in silence. My Landry is a genuine boy, for
whom life, labor, and change are all that are need-
ful; but Sylvinet has the heart of a girl, so tender
and gentle, that one cannot help loving him as the
apple of one's eye."

It was thus Mother Barbeau reasoned with herself, as she returned to her bed, but not to sleep.
Father Barbeau, in the meantime, conducted Landry across fields and meadows to Caillaud's farm
at La Priche. Arrived at the summit of a slight
hill, whence the last view of the buildings of La
Cosse could be obtained, Landry paused and
turned, his heart swelling within him as he seated
himself upon the turf, unable to proceed another
step. His father, pretending not to observe him,
walked on; but a few moments after called to him
gently, saying: "Daylight is breaking, my boy;
we must make haste if we would arrive before the
sun is up."

Landry rose, and, as he had determined not to

cry in the presence of his father, repressed the
tears which stood in his eyes, like large peas. Pretending to search for his pocket-knife, he reached
La Priche, as he thought, without betraying the
grief which overwhelmed him.

Farmer Caillaud, finding that he was to have
the strongest and most industrious of the twins,
was very glad to receive him.   He knew this separation could not have been effected without pain;
so, as he was a kind-hearted man, as well as a
great friend of Barbeau, he did his best to cheer
and encourage the lad.   He set before him some
soup, and a measure of wine to put him in heart,
for it was easy to see that he was disturbed. Then
he took him out to yoke the oxen, and praised
him for the skill he exhibited.   Landry was not a
novice at this sort of work.   His father had a fine
pair of oxen, which Landry had been accustomed
to harness and drive.   As soon as the boy saw
the large oxen of Farmer Caillaud, which were the
finest, strongest, and best fed in the country, he
felt proud to have the charge of such superb cattle.   Moreover, he was pleased to show that he
was neither awkward nor idle, and that they had
nothing new to teach him.   His father did not
fail to say a good word in his behalf, and when the
hour arrived to set out for the fields, the whole
Caillaud family, both great and small, embraced
the twin, while the youngest of the girls fastened
a bunch of flowers and ribbons to his hat, in honor
of his first day of service, which was consequently
a fête-day for the family that received him.

Before leaving, his father gave him some good counsel, in presence of his new master, desiring that he would please him in all things, and take care of his cattle as though they were his own.

Landry, having promised to do his best, went forth to his work, and, laboring well and cheerfully through the day, returned at night with a good appetite. It was his first hard day's work, and fatigue is a sovereign remedy for grief. But the day did not pass so pleasantly for poor Sylvinet. As soon as he opened his eyes, and missed his brother from his side he suspected the truth, though he could scarcely believe that Landry would depart without wishing him good-bye, and in the midst of his grief could hardly restrain a feeling of anger.

"What can I have done?" said he to his mother. "How have I displeased him? I have ever striven to do what he wished; and when he told me not to cry before you, dear mother, I forbore till my head was ready to burst. He promised not to go without a few more words of encouragement—without breakfasting with me in the hemp field, where we have so often talked and played together. I wished to put up his bundle, and to give him my knife, which is better than his own; and you must have done it for him last night, mother, without saying a word to me—knowing that he intended to go without wishing me good-bye."

"I obeyed your father," replied Mother Barbeau; at the same time doing all she could to console Sylvinet. But he refused to be comforted;

and it was not until he saw her in tears also, that
he began to caress her, and to ask pardon for having added to her sorrow, promising to remain
with and console her. But no sooner had she
left him than he ran towards La Priche, scarcely
conscious of what he was doing, and allowed himself to be carried away by that blind instinct which
sends the dove in search of its lost mate, regardless of the way.

And La Priche he would have reached had he
not met with his father, who, taking him by the
hand, said calmly:

"We will go and see Landry to-night; but you
must not disturb your brother at his work, or you
will displease his master; besides, the women at
home are in trouble, and I look to you to console
them."

CHAPTER IV.

SYLVINET returned to his mother, to cling to
her apron string like a child, and never stirred
from her side the whole day, speaking constantly
of Landry, of whom everything served to remind
him. In the evening his father accompanied him
to La Priche, fearing to trust the twins alone.
Sylvinet was almost wild with impatience to see
his brother, and, in his hurry to set out, could not
touch a morsel of supper. He felt sure Landry
would come to meet him, and kept imagining
that he saw him in the distance; but though Lan-

dry would willingly have done so, he dared not
stir, lest he should be laughed at by the boys and
girls of La Priche for this twin affection, which
they looked upon as a sort of malady.   Therefore
Sylvinet found him at table, eating and drinking
as heartily as though he had lived all his life with
the Caillauds.   But so soon as Landry saw Sylvinet his heart bounded with joy, and it was with
difficulty he could restrain himself from upsetting
table and bench to get at him the more quickly;
nevertheless, as his employers were curiously
watching him, amused with this singular affection,
this phenomenon of nature, as the schoolmaster
of the place called it, he remained seated.   When,
at last Sylvinet threw himself into his arms, embracing him with tears, and pressing him to his
bosom as a bird presses to its nest, Landry in the
midst of his own happiness could not help feeling
vexed, and, desiring to appear more reasonable
than his brother, signed to him from time to time
to restrain his feelings; a circumstance which
greatly distressed Sylvinete.   At length the two
farmers sitting down to chat over a measure of
wine, the twins effected their escape, Landry desiring to caress his brother in private.   But this
was not to be, for his young friends continued to
watch them in the distance, while Solange, the
younger daughter of Farmer Caillaud, an inquisitive and mischievous child, followed them on tip-
toe, laughing with a confused air when detected,
but never offering to turn back, in the vague ex-
pectation that she was about to witness some-

thing singular in the friendship of the two brothers, though what, she could not imagine. Sylvinet, though surprised at the tranquil air with
which his brother had met him, never dreamed of
reproaching him, so happy was he to find himself
once more by his side.

The morrow being Sunday, Landry, released
from all duty, set out for La Cosse so early in the
morning that he thought he should catch his
brother in bed. But though Sylvinet was usually
the heaviest sleeper of the two, he woke as Landry
passed through the gate of the orchard, and, as
though some instinct had told him that his twin
was approaching, ran out barefooted to meet him.
This day was to Landry one of perfect enjoyment.
He was delighted to be once more with his family,
and enjoyed it all the more that he knew it could
not be of daily occurrence, but must be looked
upon as a reward for good conduct. Sylvinet,
on his part, forgot all his sorrows till long after
day was gone. He petted his brother more ten-
derly than ever, giving him the best of everything,
the crust of his bread, and the heart of his lettuce;
and then attended to his clothes and shoes as
though Landry were going on a long journey;
and as though his twin were the one to be pitied,
without suspecting that he he was himself the real
object for sympathy, since he was the most afflicted.

A week passed thus, Sylvinet going to see Landry daily, and Landry stopping with him for a few
moments whenever he chanced to be in the neigh-

borhood of La Cosse; Landry growing more and
more reconciled to his lot, Sylvinet not reconciled
at all, but counting the days, and even the hours,
like a soul in torture.

No one in the world save Landry could induce
his brother to listen to reason; the mother, therefore, had recourse to him to tranquillize Sylvinet's
mind; still from day to day the poor boy's sorrow
increased. He could no longer play, and only
worked when commanded; and though he still
took his little sister to walk, he seldom spoke to
her or thought of answering her, simply taking
care that she did not get into mischief; and as soon
as he could make his escape, he would steal away
alone, and conceal himself so that no one could
find him. His sole consolation consisted in wandering through the lanes and meadows, where he
had been accustomed to play and chat with Landry; he would seat himself under the trees where
they had been in the habit of sitting together, and
would bathe his feet in the brooks where they had
paddled like two ducks; happy if he found a stick
fashioned by Landry, or a heap of flints which had
served them for quoits or fire-stones. These he
would gather together, concealing them in the
decayed trunk of a tree, or beneath a pile of wood,
that he might return to look at them as sacred
relics. Thus he wandered about, puzzling his
brain to retrace every trifling remembrance of
past happiness, which to any other would have appeared valueless, but which to him was all-import-
ant. Taking no heed for the future, wanting

courage to encounter the thought of a succession
of days like those he was now enduring, he lived
but in the past, absorbed in a continual dream.

At times, Sylvinet would imagine he could see
and hear his twin, and would talk to himself, as if
conversing with him. At others, he would fall
asleep, and dream of him, and, awaking, would
cry to find himself alone; making no effort to restrain his tears, because he hoped that sheer
fatigue would, in the end, abate his sufferings.
Once, wandering as far as the woods of Cham-
peaux, he suddenly came upon the dried-up chan-
nel of a spring, which in the time of heavy rains
flowed from the woods, and discovered one of
those little mills which the children of these parts
are famous for making, and which are so nicely
constructed as to turn with the current of the
water; frequently remaining for a long time, until
broken by other children, or destroyed by the
force of the stream. The one which Sylvinet now
found, had been there for more than two months,
and as the place was lonely, it had escaped all injury. He recognized it as the work of his twin,
and recollected that when it was made they
had promised themselves to return and see it, an
intention lost sight of in the construction of other
mills in different places. Sylvinet was therefore
rejoiced at this discovery, and carried the mill
down to the point whither the stream had re-
treated, that he might watch it turn, in remembrance of an amusement Landry had taught him;
and there he left it, promising himself the pleas-

ure of returning on the following Sunday, with
Landry, that he also might see how their mill had
resisted the influence of time.

But he could not abstain from returning on the
morrow, when he found the banks of the stream
disturbed and trampled down by a drove of oxen
which had come thither to drink, on their way to
graze in a neighboring thicket. Advancing a
few steps, he saw that the animals had walked
over his mill, and had so shattered it that a few
fragment^ only remained. At sight of this his
heart swelled within him; and, imagining some
mischief to his twin was connected with this accident, he ran with all speed to La Priche, to assure
himself that nothing was wrong. But as he had
observed that Landry did not like to be disturbed
at his work, lest his master should be displeased,
he contented himself with looking at him from a
distance, and made no attempt to be seen.

Sylvinet grew pale, slept badly, and ate but little; his mother became alarmed and knew not
how to treat him. She tried taking him with her
to market, and sending him to the cattle-fair with
his father and uncles; but he took no interest in
what he did; at last, his father also being alarmed,
without saying a word at home, endeavored to
persuade Farmer Caillaud to take both twins, for
a time, into his service. But this suggestion was
not kindly received.

"Suppose I were to take both as you wish; it
could not last, for in families like ours, where one
servant can do the work, two are not needed. At

the end of a year you would have to send one of these boys away, and do you not see that if Sylvinet were in service, where he was obliged to work, he would not have leisure for vain regrets, but would yield to necessity like Landry, who is as good and industrious a boy as one need desire to see. Sooner or later it must come to this; you will not always be able to find him such a place as you could wish, and, if these children are to be separated at all, the sooner it is done the better. Do not heed the caprice of a child, whom your wife and family have petted and spoiled. The most difficult step is taken, and Sylvinet will soon become reconciled, if you do not yield."

Barbeau saw the reasonableness of this, and felt that the more Sylvinet saw of his twin, the more he would desire to see. He therefore determined to procure him a situation, where, seeing less and less of Landry, he might finally acquire the habit of living like the rest of the world, and not allow himself to be overwhelmed by a restless and morbid attachment. But the time had not yet arrived to speak of this to Mother Barbeau; for, at the first hint of sending Sylvinet away, she cried herself ill, declaring he would die. Landry, by the advice of his father and master, as well as that of his mother, did his best to reconcile his twin to his fate. Sylvinet promised all that was required, but ended by finding it impossible to conquer his grief. Another feeling mingled with his sorrow, of which he never spoke—this was a devouring jealousy which had sprung up in his heart with regard to Landry.   Pleased as he was to find that every one held his brother in esteem, and that his new masters treated him as affectionately as if he were one of their own children, he could not help being grieved and distressed to see Landry, as he thought, making too ardent a return to these new friendships.   He could not endure that at Caillaud's slightest word Landry should leave father, mother, and brother, to do his bidding; more fearful of failing in his duty than in his affection, and more prompt to obey than Sylvinet would have found possible, when the remaining a few moments more with the dearest object of his affection was in question.

Thus, this poor child cherished a sorrow which he had never before experienced, in the belief that the love was all on his side—that his affection was but ill requited—and that this must have been the case from the first, though he had never suspected it; unless indeed the love of his twin had, of late, grown colder, since he had met elsewhere persons who pleased and suited him better.

CHAPTER V.

LANDRY could not understand this jealousy in his brother.   Therefore, when Sylvinet came to visit him, Landry, thinking to amuse him, took him to see the large oxen, the fine cows, and abundant crops of Farmer Caillaud, for Landry valued

all these, not from pride, but from a natural taste
for agricultural labor. Thus, he took pleasure in
seeing the colt which he had to lead to the meadow, fat, clean and glossy, and he could not endure that whatever was worth doing at all should
be done badly. Sylvinet viewed all these matters
with indifference, and was surprised that his
brother should take so much interest in what did
not concern him. He was, in fact, dissatisfied,
and said to Landry:

"You seem greatly taken with these large cattle, and no longer give a thought to our little
oxen, so full of life and courage, and yet so gentle
and affectionate to us, that they would always
allow themselves to be yoked more willingly by
you than by our father. You have not even
asked me after our cow, which gives us such good
milk, and which, poor beast, looks at me with so
sad an air when I take her food to her, as if she
understood that I was alone, and would ask me
after my brother."

"It is true she is a good beast," said Landry,
"but look at these! you shall see them milked, and
then you will say you never in your life saw so
much milk given at a time."

"That may be," returned Sylvinet, "but that the
milk and the cream are as good as the milk and
the cream of our brown cow you will never get me
to believe; for the grass of La Bessonnière is better than the grass here."

"Indeed!" said Landry, "and yet I believe my
father would gladly make the exchange, if he

could have the fat hay of Farmer Caillaud for that of his, which grows on the borders of the stream, and which is not a little injured by the rushes."

"Bah!" replied Sylvinet, shrugging his shoulders; "there are in that same meadow much finer trees than all yours put together; and, as for the hay, if it be not so abundant, it is finer, and as it is carried home leaves a balmy odor wherever it passes."

Thus did the twins dispute about nothing, for Landry knew that there is no greater blessing than contentment; while Sylvinet had no especial regard for his own possessions over those of La Priche, spite of the abuse he heaped upon them. But at the bottom of all this vain contention there was on the one side a lad content to work and live, no matter where or how; and on the other an unfortunate boy who could not understand how his brother should know a moment of pleasure apart from him.

If Landry led him into his master's garden, and while chatting stopped to cut a dead branch from a tree or to pull up a weed from the vegetables, Sylvinet was vexed to find his brother full of his duty to others, instead of being devoted to himself. He did not, however, suffer any of this feeling to appear; but at the moment of quitting Landry he would sometimes say:

"There, you have had quite enough of me for to-day. It may be you have had too much, and find my visits tedious."

Landry could not comprehend these reproach-

3

es, yet they caused him pain; and in his turn he reproached his brother, who neither could nor would explain.

If the poor child were jealous of the slightest thing which occupied Landry's attention, he was still more jealous of the persons for whom Landry evinced attachment.   He could not endure that his   ner should be intimate with the boys of La l   ne; and when he saw him amusing or caressing the little Solange, he reproached him with forgetting his sister Nanette, who, according to him, was a thousand times prettier and more interesting than "that ugly child!"

But as justice is incompatible with jealousy, when Landry came to La Bessonière then Sylvinet thought he appeared too much engrossed with Nanette, and reproached him with paying attention to no one but her, and for his utter indifference to himself.

In short, his affection became by degrees so exacting, his temper so morose, that Landry began to suffer and to find that it was no longer for his happiness to see his brother too often.   He was weary of hearing himself forever reproached for yielding so readily to his fate; by which reproaches one would have thought Sylvinet would have felt happier if he could have first rendered his brother as miserable as himself.   Landry understood, and wished to make him understand, how an affection carried to excess may sometimes become a misfortune.   Sylvinet would not listen to such an argument, and even considered it a great wrong that his brother should entertain such an idea. At last he would pass whole weeks without going to La Priche, all the time dying to see Landry, but restraining himself from a false feeling of pride. At length it came to pass that from words to words, from vexations to vexations, Sylvinet, always misunderstanding what Landry said to him, arrived at such a state of indignation that at times he fancied he hated the object of so much love; and, one Sunday in particular, quitted the house that he might not pass the day with his brother, who never once failed to devote the Sabbath to his service.

Such childish perverseness greatly chagrined Landry. Growing every day more manly, it was natural he should love pleasure and excitement. In all games of skill he was sure to be first, the most supple of body, the quickest of eye. It was therefore no slight sacrifice he offered his brother in leaving the joyous lads of La Priche every Sunday to pass the whole day at La Bessonnière; for Sylvinet, who had remained much more of a child in mind than Landry, and who had but one idea, that of loving and being loved devotedly, desired nothing better than that his brother should repair with him alone to the haunts where they used to amuse themselves with games no longer suitable to their age—such as making wheelbarrows of rushes, and little mills or building houses with stones, and laying out fields as large as a pocket handkerchief, which they pretended to cultivate in divers manners, imitating the laborers whom they saw

ploughing, sowing and reaping, thus teaching
each other in an hour's time all the modes of culti-
vation and tilling which occupy the cycle of the
year. These amusements were no longer to the
taste of Landry, who would have preferred playing at ninepins with the big boys of the neighborhood, in which game he was an adept; but if, by
chance, Sylvinet consented to accompany him, instead of joining in the game he would sit in a corner and never open his lips, ready to fret and torment when Landry appeared to enter into the
game with zeal and pleasure.

Landry had learned to dance at La Priche; he
was esteemed a good dancer of the bourrée, and
though yet too young to care for kissing the girls,
according to the custom of this dance, he was content to follow the general example, all the more
willingly as it seemed to announce his emancipa-
tion from childhood; and he would not have been
displeased had the girls offered the same resistance to him as to the men. But he had not yet
achieved this distinction, and even the oldest
among them would catch him, laughing, round
the neck, at the risk of no small offence to his dignity.

Sylvinet had once seen him dance, and it had
been the cause of his greatest vexation, for he was
so enraged to see him kiss one of Caillaud's
daughters that he wept with jealousy and pronounced the whole thing indecent. Thus, while
yielding his own amusements to the affection of
his brother, Landry did not pass very pleasant

Sabbaths; still, he had never once absented himself, thinking that Sylvinet would appreciate the sacrifice, and lost sight of his own disappointment in the thought of giving happiness to his brother.

When, therefore, he found that Sylvinet, who had been moody through the week, had quitted the house that he might not see him, he in his turn was vexed, and for the first time since he had left his family gave way to tears, taking care, however, to conceal himself, from a mingled feeling of shame and a desire to spare his parents additional grief.

If either of them had a right to be jealous it was Landry, since Sylvinet was the darling of the mother; and even Barbeau, though entertaining a secret preference for Landry, showed most consideration for his brother. This poor lad, being the weaker and the least reasonable of the two, was also the most spoiled. At the same time his fate was the easier, inasmuch as he remained with his family, while Landry had to endure separation and toil.

For the first time our good Landry, thus reasoning within himself, came to the conclusion that the conduct of his twin was altogether unjust. Until then his kind heart had prevented his thinking him in the wrong; and, rather than accuse him, he had condemned himself for possessing too much health and strength, and for wanting the gentle manners and disposition of his brother. But this time he could find in himself no sin against their affection. He had given up a fish-

ing party with the lads of La Priche which promised much pleasure, that he might pass the day
with his twin; and, at his age, it is no small thing
to resist such a temptation. In the midst of his
weeping he was suddenly arrested by the voice of
some one near him, evidently in great distress,
and talking to themselves, after the custom of
country women when overwhelmed with sorrow.
Landry quickly recognized the voice of his mother
and hastened to her.

"Alas!" said she to herself, sobbing, "why must
that child cause me so much sorrow? He will be
the death of me, I am sure!"

"Is it I, mother, who am the cause of your sorrow?" exclaimed Landry. "If it be, punish me,
but do not weep. I know not how I can have
grieved you, but I beg forgiveness all the same."

At this moment the mother knew that Landry
had not a hard heart, as she had often imagined.
She smiled, kissed him fervently, and, scarcely
knowing what she said in her distress, told him it
was Sylvinet of whom she complained; that it was
true she had sometimes entertained a harsh
thought against him, for which she now offered
reparation; but that Sylvinet appeared to her to
be going out of his senses, and that she was uneasy at his departing before daylight, without
breaking his fast. The sun was now beginning
to decline, and still he did not return. He had
been last seen by the side of the river, and the unhappy mother feared he might have thrown himself in to put an end to his days.

CHAPTER VI.

THE idea that Sylvinet might have destroyed himself passed from the mind of the mother to that of Landry as easily as a fly enters the web of a spider; and, filled with grief, he lost no time in seeking for his brother, saying to himself as he went along: "Perhaps my mother was right when she reproached me for being hard-hearted on former occasions; but just now Sylvinet must be cruel indeed to give such pain to poor mother and me."

He ran hither and thither, calling aloud upon his name, but receiving no reply; and asking all whom he met if they could give him any news of his brother. At last, finding himself to the right of the meadow bordering on the stream, he entered, remembering that it contained a nook to which Sylvinet was very partial. This was a large gap which the river had made in one of the banks by washing down two or three trees, which in their fall had lodged across the stream, their roots in the air. Farmer Barbeau, sacrificing the timber, had left them undisturbed, as, from the manner in which they lay, the earth still clinging to the roots, they offered an effectual resistance to the water, which every winter made much havoc, stealing a piece from the meadow.

Landry approached this cleft, and, instead of giving himself time to turn the corner, where, with

their own hands, they had constructed a flight of
steps from clods of turf, stones, and roots of trees,
he sprang at once as far down as he could, that he
might arrive the more quickly at the bottom, since
on the right bank of the ravine the undergrowth
was so thick that, supposing his brother to be
there, he could not see him without descending.

Landry entered in great emotion; for ever in
his mind was the idea suggested by his mother
that Sylvinet had put an end to his days.   He
passed and repassed among the foliage, beating
the bushes in all directions, calling Sylvinet, whistling to the dog who had doubtless followed him,
since neither he nor his young master had been
seen at the house through the day.

But Landry might have searched and called for
ever; he was alone in the cleft.   He examined
both banks in search of footmarks, or such disturbance of the ground as might indicate the
whereabouts of his brother.   It was a perplexing
search, for it was more than a month since Landry
had been in that spot; and, had he known it as he
knew his own hand, it was impossible but some
change must have taken place.   The right bank
was covered with grass; indeed, the whole of the
cleft was so overgrown with rushes that not a corner was to be found where the trace of a footmark
might be left.   At length, after a long search,
Landry discovered the track of a dog; and further
on a spot where the leaves were crushed, as
though Feriot, or some other dog of his size, had
there curled himself round to sleep.

This only increased his alarm, and he proceeded afresh to examine the high bank of the river, where he fancied he could detect a recent mark, as if made by the foot of a person springing or sliding down; and though this might easily have been the work of one of those large water-rats with which such places abound, he was so terrified that, his limbs failing him, he fell upon his knees and commended himself to God.

At length the idea occurred to him to go and consult Mother Fadet, a learned woman who resided at the end of the meadow, close to the road which leads to the ford. This woman, who had no other property than her little garden and house, did not find it necessary to work for her living, inasmuch as her knowledge of the troubles and disasters of this world had established so famous a repute that people came from all quarters to consult her. Equally celebrated was she for secret and mysterious cures of wounds, sprains, and other maladies of the kind; and for not a little of the faith reposed in her was she indebted to the cure of diseases which never existed.

But, for the valuable remedies with which she was in reality acquainted, for her sovereign plasters for cuts and burns, for the drinks which she composed to allay fever, there is no doubt she earned her money honestly, and that many sick people were cured when the doctor's drugs would have killed. At least she said so, and those whom she had saved preferred taking her word to risking the consequences of unbelief. As in the country all knowledge is held to be sorcery, many thought that Mother Fadet knew more than she cared to own; and to her was therefore attributed the power of finding lost things and persons; in short, as her superior judgment and cleverness enabled her to assist people out of their troubles, where it was possible, they inferred that she could do it where it was not.

All children listen eagerly to marvellous stories. Landry heard it said that Mother Fadet, by means of certain seed which she threw upon the water, at the same time muttering a few words, could cause the body of a drowned person to be found. The seed, thus prepared, floated with the current of the water, and there where it was seen to stop the body was sure to be discovered. Landry ran to the cottage of Mother Fadet, related his trouble and begged her to return to the cleft to find his brother, living or dead.

Now, Mother Fadet, who did not like to see her reputation endangered, and who never willingly exercised her talent for nothing, not only jeered at poor Landry, but drove him harshly away. She had been dissatisfied in times past because La Sagette had been employed in her place in the Barbeau family. Landry, who was naturally proud, would perhaps at any other time have been angry, though he was now so overwhelmed and distressed that he said not a word, but returned to the cleft, determined to prosecute his search in the water, though he neither knew how to dive nor to swim. But as he was walking along, his head bowed down and his eyes fixed upon the ground, he felt some one tap him on the shoulder, and, turning, beheld the grand-daughter of Mother Fadet, called in those parts the little Fadette, partly because it was her family name, and partly because people would have it that she also was somewhat of a sorceress. Now, *fadet*, or *farfadet*, which in some places is also called *follet*, is a hobgoblin, harmless, but given to mischief and fun. People often mistook little Fadette for one of those spirits, so small, thin, weather-beaten and dishevelled did she appear; lively as a butterfly, curious as a robin-redbreast, and dark as a cricket.

Now, when I compare the little Fadette to a cricket, it is to let you know that she was not handsome, for this poor little insect of the fields is even more ugly than that of the hearthstone. Still, if ever as a child you remember having played with one, you ought to know that it has by no means a stupid or unmeaning countenance, but one more likely to provoke laughter than tears: thus, the children of La Cosse, who are as quick as others in discerning likenesses and drawing comparisons, called little Fadette the Cricket, whenever they wished to enrage her, and sometimes even by way of kindness; for they stood in some little fear of her, and did not altogether despise her, because she told them long stories, and taught them new games of her own invention.

But all these names and surnames make me almost forget that which she had received at her

baptism, and which the reader may perhaps desire
hereafter to know.   She was called Francoise,
and therefore her grandmother, who did not approve of nicknames, always called her Fanchon.

As for some time past there had been a feud
between the family of La Bessonnière and Mother
Fadet, the twins never spoke much to Fanchon;
they even entertained, as it were, an aversion for
her, and never willingly played either with her or
her brother the Grasshopper, as he was called,
who, still more cunning and mischievous than
herself, was always at her side, getting into a rage
when she ran too fast for him, throwing stones at
her when she mocked him, and often enraging
her more than she desired, since she was of a gay
humor, and disposed to treat everything as a jest.
But such strange notions prevailed concerning
Mother Fadet, that many children, and more especially those of Farmer Barbeau, imagined that
the Cricket and the Grasshopper would bring misfortune upon them in any intimacy they might
form.   This fear, however, was not so strong as
to prevent their talking together whenever they
met; for, as we have said, the twins were not bashful, and Fanchon seldom failed to accost them
with all kinds of jokes and nonsense as soon as
she saw them approach.

CHAPTER VII.

When Landry, turning round in indignation at the blow he had just received on the shoulder, saw Fanchon, and, limping after her, Jeanot the Grasshopper, lame from his birth, he felt disposed to pay no attention, and to continue his road in silence, but Fanchon, tapping him on the other shoulder, said: "Ah, ah! you stupid twin! you half of a boy, who has lost his other half!"

Upon this, Landry, who was in no humor to be teased, turned again, and aimed a blow at Fanchon, which, fortunately, she avoided. The Cricket was much too nimble and alert to wait for blows, and made up in agility and cunning for what she lacked in strength. Upon this occasion she sprung aside so suddenly that Landry all but found himself, fist and nose, with a large tree which stood by.

"You wicked Cricket!" exclaimed the poor twin in anger, "you must indeed be heartless when you can provoke any one in such trouble as I am. You have teased me for some time, by calling me the half of a boy; I have a great mind now to break you and your mischievous Grasshopper into four quarters, to see if, between you, you will make the fourth part of anything good!"

"So, so, my fine twin, heir of the meadow on the border of the river," replied Fanchon, still laughing; "you are very foolish to quarrel with

me, when I come to give you news of your brother
and to tell you where to find him."

"Oh, that alters the case," said Landry, quickly
pacified. "If you do know anything about him,
Fanchon, tell me quickly, and I shall be grateful."

"Neither Fanchon nor the Cricket cares for
your gratitude, just now," replied the little girl.
"You have said bad things, and you would have
struck me had you been less heavy and clumsy.
So you may seek for your fool of a twin, since you
know how to set about it so cleverly."

"I am very foolish to listen to you at all, you
bad girl," said Landry, turning his back and continuing his walk. "You know no more than I do
where my brother is, for you are no wiser in
these matters than your grandmother, who is an
old story-teller, and a cheat into the bargain."

But Fanchon, seizing her Grasshopper by the
hair, who by this time had managed to overtake
and hang on to her dirty petticoat, followed Landry, still laughing, and declaring that, without her
assistance, he would never find his twin.   Landry, being unable to get rid of her, and imagining
that, by some witchcraft, her grandmother, or
perhaps even she herself, through her intimacy
with the will-o'-the-wisp, might prevent him from
finding Sylvinet, determined to give up the search
and return home.   Fanchon followed him as far
as the stile leading to the meadow, and, when he
had got over it, perched herself like a magpie on
the top, and cried after him:

"Good-bye, you heartless twin! So, you are

content to leave your brother behind you! You need not wait for him at supper; you will not see him to-day; no, nor to-morrow, either; for he will no more move from where he now is than a stone; and a storm is coming on. There will be more trees blown into the river to-night, and the stream will carry Sylvinet so far away that you will never be able to find him again."

These wicked words, which Landry could not help hearing, sent a cold thrill through his frame. He did not exactly believe all she said; but still the Fadettes were reported to have such an understanding with the Prince of Darkness that he could not feel assured they were wholly devoid of truth.

"Come, Fanchon," said Landry, stopping, "yes or no; will you leave me in peace, or will you tell me truly whether you know anything about my brother?"

"And what will you give me if, before the rain begins to fall, I enable you to find him?" said Fanchon, standing upright on the stile, and shaking her arms as though she were about to fly.

Landry knew not what to promise, and began to think that her object was to get money out of him. But the wind whistled among the trees, and the thunder began to rumble, filling him with feverish apprehension.

"Fanchon," said he, "if you will restore my brother to me I will do whatever you wish. Perhaps you have seen him, and know where he is. Be a good girl. I cannot imagine why you should take pleasure in my distress. Show me that you have a kind heart, and henceforth I will believe you to be better than your words and manner imply."

"And why should I be a good girl for your sake," said she, "when you ill-treat me, though I never did you any harm? Why should I do a kindness for a couple of twins, who are as proud as fighting-cocks, and who have never shown me the slightest consideration?"

"Come, Fanchon," returned Landry, "you wish me to promise you something; tell me at once what you desire, and I will give it to you. Will you have my new knife?"

"Let me see it," said Fanchon, hopping like a frog to his side.

Now, when she saw the knife, which was an excellent one, and a present from Landry's god-father at the last fair, she was, for a moment, tempted; but, soon thinking this was not enough, she asked him if, instead, he would give her his little white chicken, which was no bigger than a pigeon, and had feathers to the end of its toes.

"I cannot promise you the chicken, because it is my mother's," returned Landry; "but I will promise to ask if you may have it, and I will undertake that I shall not be refused, since my mother will be only too glad to see Sylvinet, and will think nothing too much to give you in return."

"Indeed!" said Fanchon; "suppose I were to

ask for the black-nosed goat; would Mother Barbeau give me that also?"

"Oh, how long you are in deciding, Fanchon!
Stay, one word is enough; if my brother be in
danger, and you will take me to him immediately,
you can ask neither for hen, chicken, goat or kid,
which my folks will not willingly give you."

"Well, we shall see, Landry," said Fanchon,
holding out her small dry hand to the twin, that
he might take it in token of compact, which he
did, but not without trembling, for at that moment her eyes were so brilliant that she looked
like the will-o'-the-wisp in person. "I shall not
tell you now what I will have, perhaps I have not
quite made up my own mind; but remember what
you have promised, for should you break your
word, I will tell every one that there is no reliance to be placed on the honor of twin Landry.   So good-bye to you here, and do not forget
that I shall not remind you of my claim, until the
day when I shall require from you something
which must be at my command, and which you
shall yield without hesitation or regret."

"So be it, Fanchon, it is a promise," said Landry, pressing her hand.

"Go," said she, with a proud and satisfied air,
"return by this path to the bank of the river; then
descend until you hear a bleating, and where you
find a lamb, there will you also find your brother.
If everything does not come to pass as I say, I
hold you quit of your promise."

Thereupon the Cricket, taking the Grasshopper

4

beneath her arm, whether he liked it or not,
sprung right into the middle of a neighboring
thicket, and Landry heard and saw no more of
the pair than if he had only been dreaming. However, losing no time in considering whether Fanchon was deceiving him or not, he ran with all
speed to the meadow, and was about to pass the
cleft, which he had already searched, when he
heard the bleating of a lamb.

"Good Heaven!" thought he, "this girl foretold
truly; I hear the lamb, therefore my brother is
there, but whether dead or alive, I know not."

Landry sprung down the cleft, and entered
among the brambles. His brother was not to be
seen; but following the course of the stream for
about ten paces, the lamb still continuing to bleat,
Landry saw seated upon the opposite bank his
brother, holding in his blouse a young lamb, covered with mud from the tip of its nose to the end
of its tail.

On finding Sylvinet alive, and, to all appearance, unhurt, Landry was so overcome with joy
that he poured out his thanks to Heaven, without
thinking of asking forgiveness for owing his happiness to a sorceress.

As he was about to call Sylvinet, who had not
yet perceived him, and who did not appear conscious of his approach, he paused to look at him
once more, and was astonished to find him, as
Fanchon had predicted, sitting, motionless as a
stone, among the trees, which the wind was vio-
lently agitating.

Fatigued with his aimless wanderings through the day, there he sat like the stump of a tree, his eyes fixed on the flowing stream, his face pale as the water-lily, his mouth half open, like a fish gasping in the sun, his hair disordered by the wind; utterly regardless of the lamb which he had found straying in the field, and on which he had taken pity, placing it in his blouse to carry it back to its dam, though he had forgotten to inquire on his way to whom the lost lamb belonged. It was resting on his knees, its cries disregarded, though the poor little thing bleated in a voice of despair, and gazed around with its large clear eyes, astonished at not being heard by some of its species, and looking in vain in this gloomy and rush-grown spot, by the side of a rapid current of water, which, perhaps, added not a little to its terror, for its meadow, its mother and its fold.

CHAPTER VIII.

HAD not Landry been separated from Sylvinet by the river, he would assuredly have sprung to the arms of his brother without further reflection. But as Sylvinet did not even see him, he had time to think of the manner in which he should arouse him from his reverie and induce him to return home; for, as it was, should this proposition not meet the wishes of the poor sulky lad, he could easily withdraw, before Landry could find a ford to rejoin him.   Landry, therefore, after a moment or two of reflection, bethought himself how his father, who had the good sense and prudence of four men, would proceed under similar circumstances, and he decided that Farmer Barbeau would take the matter coolly, so as to conceal from Sylvinet the misery he had caused, that he might neither excite too lively a repentance, nor encourage him, on some future occasion of temper, to try the same freak again.

He began, therefore, to whistle, as though inviting the blackbirds and thrushes to sing, upon which Sylvinet raised his head, and being ashamed at the sight of his brother, rose hastily, believing he had not been seen.   Then Landry pretended to observe him for the first time, and said, without raising his voice, for the river was not so loud but that he could be heard: "Ah, Sylvinet, are you there?   I have been waiting for you all the morning, but you stayed so long that I came here to walk till supper, expecting to find you at home on my return; but since you are here we will go back together.   Let us descend the stream on our opposite banks till we meet at the ford of Roulettes."

This was the ford to the right of Mother Fadet's cottage.

"Come on, then," said Sylvinet, taking the lamb in his arms, as, upon so short an acquaintance, it could scarcely be expected to follow him."

And thus they descended the river, neither looking at the other, lest he should betray the grief it

caused him to be on bad terms, and the pleasure
he felt at this reconciliation. From time to time,
that he might not appear to be thinking of his
brother's anger, Landry addressed a word or two
to him as they walked on. And, first, he asked
him where he had found his stray lamb; to which
question, simple as it was, Sylvinet found it difficult to reply, since he did not wish to confess
how far he had been, and knew not himself the
names of the different places he had passed
through. Landry perceiving his embarrassment,
continued: "You shall tell me all about it bye
and bye, for the wind is high, and it is not quite
safe to be under the trees so close to the water;
fortunately the rain is beginning to fall, so the
wind will fall also." While he thought to himself,
the Cricket was right when she told me I should
find him before the rain began; certainly, that girl
is wiser than the rest of us.

He forgot that he had passed a good quarter of
an hour in explanation and entreaty with Mother
Fadet and that he met Fanchon on leaving the
house, so that in the meantime she might easily
have seen Sylvinet. This idea did at last occur to
him; but, then, how had she been able to divine
the cause of his trouble, when there had been no
time for an explanation with the old woman?
The thought never suggested itself that he had
already asked several persons after his brother,
and that some among them might have spoken of
it before Fanchon; or that the little girl might
possibly have overheard the close of his conversa-

tion with the grandmother, concealing herself, as
she was accustomed to do, whenever she desired
to satisfy her curiosity.

Sylvinet, in the meantime, was thinking to himself how he should explain his bad conduct to his
mother and brother, for he never suspected the
part Landry was playing, and knew not what
story to invent in justification, for he had never
told a falsehood in his life, and hitherto had concealed nothing from his twin.

As he passed the ford his embarrassment increased, for he had come thus far without being
able to devise any means of getting out of his
difficulty. As soon as he reached the bank where
his brother stood, Landry embraced him in spite
of himself, with more warmth than usual, but he
forbore all question, seeing that Sylvinet knew
not what to reply, and conducted him home,
speaking on all subjects but that which was nearest the hearts of both. As they passed the cottage of Mother Fadet, Landry endeavored to get
sight of Fanchon, for he felt a great desire to offer
her his thanks, but the door was closed and no
sound was to be heard save the voice of the
Grasshopper, crying because his grandmother
had flogged him, as she did every night, whether
he deserved it or not.

It pained Sylvinet to hear the unfortunate
urchin cry, and he said to his brother:

"That is a wicked house; pass when you will,
blows and cries are always to be heard. I know
there can be nothing more mischievous and pro-

voking than the Grasshopper, and as for the
Cricket, she is no better. But still these poor
children are to be pitied for having neither father
nor mother and for being dependent upon this old
witch, who is always in a bad temper and who
makes no allowance for their faults."

"It was not thus in our home," replied Landry.
"Never did we receive the slightest blow from
father or mother, and when they corrected us for
our childish folly it was done with such kindness
and gentleness that the neighbors knew nothing
about it. Yet others as fortunate as ourselves do
not always value their blessings, while this Fanchon, who is the most miserable and ill-treated
child upon earth, is ever merry and free from complaint."

Sylvinet understood the reproach and repented
his errors. He had repented before since morning, and twenty times over had felt tempted to
return, but shame had withheld him. Now, his
heart being full, he wept without saying a word.
His brother took him by the hand, saying:

"This is a heavy rain, Sylvinet; let us run
home."

They set off, Landry trying to make Sylvinet
laugh, who did his best to second him. But as
they were entering the house, Sylvinet felt a great
desire to run and hide himself in the barn, for he
dreaded the reproaches of his father. But Barbeau did not take things so seriously as his wife,
and contented himself with laughing at Sylvinet,
while Mother Barbeau, by the advice of her hus-

band, tried to conceal the anxiety she had felt.
However, as she was drying their clothes before a
good fire and giving the twins their supper, Sylvinet could not help seeing that she had been crying, and that from time to time she looked at him
with an uneasy and sorrowful air.   Had they
been alone he would at once have implored her
forgivenesss and have caressed her back to happiness, but the father was no great admirer of
these endearments, and Sylvinet, overcome with
fatigue, was obliged to go to bed immediately
after supper without saying a word to his mother.
Having eaten nothing during the day, he had no
sooner swallowed his meal, of which he stood in
need, than he felt as though he were intoxicated,
and was obliged to allow himself to be undressed
and put to bed by his brother, who remained by
his side, holding his hand in his own.

As soon as he saw he was asleep, Landry took
leave of his parents, but without perceiving that
his mother embraced him more affectionately
than usual.   He always thought she did not love
him as well as she loved his brother, but this did
not make him jealous, as he believed himself less
attractive and was satisfied that he got his due.
He was therefore resigned both from respect for
his mother and from affection for his twin, who,
more than himself, needed caresses and tenderness.   The next morning Sylvinet ran to the bedside of his mother and confessed his sorrow and
his shame.   He told her how unhappy he had
been for some time past, not only at separation

from Landry, but because he imagined Landry no longer loved him. And when his mother reasoned with him upon this injustice he was unable to defend himself for what was in fact a malady. The mother sympathized with him more than she was willing to show, for the heart of a woman is peculiarly susceptible to such emotions, and she had herself suffered in Landry's tranquil devotion and courage. But now she perceived that jealousy is bad in all affections, even in those which God enjoins upon us the most strictly, and she took care not to encourage this passion in Sylvinet. She showed him the pain he had caused his brother and Landry's goodness in neither complaining nor taking offence. Sylvinet readily assented and acknowledged that his brother was a better Christian than himself. He promised and resolved to amend, and his will was sincere. But in spite of himself, though he endeavored to appear consoled and satisfied, though his mother had done her best to soothe and reassure him, and though he himself did all he could to act calmly and justly towards his brother, a leaven of bitterness remained in his heart.

"My brother," thought he, "is the most Christian of us two; my dear mother says so and I feel it to be true, yet if he loved me as I love him he could not submit to our separation as he does."

And thereupon he thought of the tranquil and almost indifferent air Landry had assumed when he found him on the bank of the river. He remembered how he had heard him whistling to the birds as he prosecuted his search, at the very moment, too, when he was indeed thinking of throwing himself into the river. For if this had not been his idea when he quitted the house, it had occurred to him more than once as the day advanced, in the belief that his brother would never forgive him for having avoided him for the first time in his life.

"Had he offered me this affront," thought he, "I should have been inconsolable. I am glad he has forgiven me, but still I should not have thought he could overlook it so readily."

Thus this unfortunate child sighed as he struggled against his jealousy, and reproaching himself as he sighed, struggled afresh. But as God ever assists those who sincerely desire to please Him, by degrees Sylvinet became more reasonable, so that for the rest of the year he abstained from sulking and quarrelling with his brother, whom, to all appearance, he loved more tranquilly, while his health, which had suffered in these violent emotions, improved and strengthened. His father also required him to work more, finding that the less he was indulged the better he was in health and spirits. But home work is never so severe as that exacted by strangers. Thus Landry, who never thought of sparing himself, gained more strength and grew more manly in the year than his brother. The slight difference which from the first had existed between them now became more marked, and from their minds passed into their countenances. Landry at fifteen was a fine, handsome lad; Sylvinet a pretty youth, smaller and less robust than his brother. They could be no longer taken for each other, and though the resemblance at first sight was still strong, they would scarcely have been thought twins. Landry, who was in fact the younger, being born exactly one hour after his twin, looked to be a year or two older, and this increased his father's affection for him, who, like most country people, esteemed size and strength before all else.

CHAPTER IX.

For the first few days after Landry's adventure with Fanchon he felt uneasy at the recollection of the promise he had made, since, in the distress of the moment, he had engaged for his father and mother to give her whatever she liked best at La Bessonnière; and now, when he came to reflect, Barbeau had shown so little anxiety concerning Sylvinet's disappearance that when Fanchon should come to claim her reward he feared lest his father should shut the door in her face, ridiculing both her pretended science and the promise Landry had made.

This fear filled Landry with shame, and in proportion as his grief and terror subsided, he blamed himself for his folly in believing that witchcraft had anything to do with what had occurred. He did not altogether believe that Fan-

chon had imposed upon him, though he saw that
the transaction was open to a doubt, and he could
find no good reasons to give his father for having
undertaken an engagement of such importance;
while, on the other hand, he did not see how he
could break a promise made in all faith and sin-
cerity.

To his great surprise, neither on the morrow of
this adventure, nor the day after, nor through the
whole week, month, or season, did he hear anything of Fanchon. Neither did she present herself to Farmer Caillaud, asking to speak to Landry, nor to Farmer Barbeau, claiming her reward;
and if Landry saw her at a distance in the fields she
never sought him, or appeared to pay any attention to his presence, contrary to all custom, since
she was fond of running after every one, either
from an idle curiosity, or for the sake of playing
and joking with those who were in good humor,
or teasing and rallying those who were not.

The house of Mother Fadet being situated between La Priche and La Cosse, it could not but
happen, sooner or later, that Landry should find
himself face to face with Fanchon; and the road
being narrow, a tap on the shoulder, or a word in
passing, would be unavoidable.

One evening, when Fanchon was driving home
her geese, and Landry, who had been to fetch the
mares from the field, was quietly leading them to
La Priche, this encounter took place in a bye-
road which, lying between two high banks, offered no means of escape. At the thought of

being called upon to redeem his promise Landry
grew red in the face, and, unwilling to give Fanchon the slightest encouragement, as soon as he
saw her, jumped on the back of one of the mares
and began plying it with his heels to induce it to
trot; but, as the mares had blocks attached to their
legs, the poor beast went none the faster for this
summary application to her sides. Landry, finding
himself close upon Fanchon and not daring to look
her in the face, turned round as if to see that the
colts were following, and when he again looked forward Fanchon had passed on without saying a
word, nor could he even tell whether she had looked
at him, and by her eyes or smile had solicited a
good evening. Jeanot the Grasshopper only remained, who, ever full of mischief, took up a stone
to throw at the mare Landry was riding. Landry
felt greatly tempted to give him a blow with his
whip, but fearing that by so doing he should provoke an explanation with the sister, he affected not
to perceive the mischievous urchin and went on
his way without ever looking behind him. Every
time Landry and Fanchon met he behaved in the
same manner, till by degrees he grew bold enough
to look her in the face, since, as he grew older, he
ceased to be uneasy about so trifling an affair.
When at last he had taken courage to look at and
speak to her, he was astonished to find that the
girl herself studiously turned her head to one side,
as though she entertained the same fear of him as
he had formerly entertained of her. This embold-
ened him all the more, and as he was of a just and

an upright disposition, he asked himself whether he had not done wrong in never thanking her for the service which, by skill or chance, she had really rendered him. He determined, therefore, to speak to her the next time he saw her, and that time having arrived, he took at least ten steps out of his way to say good morning.

But, as he approached, Fanchon assumed a proud and dignified air; and when at last she deigned to look at him, it was with so contemptuous an expression that Landry was taken aback and dared not utter a word.

This was the last time in that year Landry met her, for from that day Fanchon, from some unaccountable fancy, avoided him so scrupulously that when she saw him in the distance she would turn another way, or take a circuit, that she might not meet him. Landry thought she was displeased at the ingratitude he had shown, but his repugnance towards her was so great that he could not make up his mind to offer any atonement. Fanchon was unlike other children. She was not naturally disposed to take offence; indeed, she was frequently reproached with wanting the pride becoming to a girl of her age, and would often provoke sneers and insults, conscious that she should have the best of the encounter and be sure to come off with the last and most stinging word. Sulkiness formed no part of her disposition. She had all the tricks of a mischievous boy, and loved to torment Sylvinet whenever she happened to surprise him in one of his reveries, to which he was

still at times addicted; following his steps, laughing at his twinship, and telling him that Landry no
longer loved him, and was even amused at his sorrow.   Poor Sylvinet, still more disposed than
Landry to look upon her as a witch, marvelled
that she should divine his thoughts, and hated her
cordially.   He despised both her and her family;
and as the Cricket avoided Landry, so did Sylvinet
avoid the wicked Cricket, saying that, sooner or
later, she would follow the example of her mother
and come to a bad end.

Her mother, soon after the birth of the Grasshopper, deserted her husband to follow the soldiers as a *vivandiere.*   The husband had died of
grief and shame; upon which the two children fell
to the care of Mother Fadet, who, too old herself
to attend to them properly, and too stingy to go
to any expense on their account. left them to
grow up as they might.

For these reasons even Landry, who was more
her friend than his brother, entertained a feeling
of aversion towards Fanchon, and regretting that
he had had anything to do with her, he took care
not to let any one else into the secret.   He even
concealed it from his twin, being unwilling to confess the anxiety he had felt on his account; while
Sylvinet concealed from Landry the mischievous
conduct of Fanchon towards himself, being
ashamed to confess that she had divined his unaccountable jealousy.

But time passed on.   At the age our twins had
now reached, weeks are equivalent to months,

months to years, for the change which they bring
both to mind and body. Landry quickly forgot
his adventure and thought no more of Fanchon
than if the whole occurrence had been a dream.

It was more than ten months after Landry had
taken service at La Priche, and the fête of St. John
(or, as we call it, midsummer), the epoch of his
engagement with Farmer Caillaud, was fast approaching. Now the farmer was so satisfied with
Landry that he had already made up his mind to
increase his wages rather than lose him, while
Landry desired nothing better than to remain in
the vicinity of his family and to renew his engagement with the people of La Priche, who suited
him admirably. It is not necessary to determine
how far Landry was influenced in this desire by
a growing partiality for a niece of Farmer Caillaud, called Madelon, who was the belle of the village. A year older than Landry, she still treated
him somewhat like a child; a feeling, however,
which was daily diminishing, inasmuch as at the
beginning of the year she had laughed at him for
being ashamed to kiss her at the conclusion of the
bourree, she now blushed as she received the sa-
lute, and would no longer remain alone with him
in the stable or hayloft. Madelon did not want
for means, and a marriage between the young
couple might easily be arranged hereafter. The
two families were equally well off; equally esteemed by their neighbors. In short, Caillaud,
fancying he saw symptoms of a growing attachment, took an opportunity of saying to Barbeau

that they would make a handsome couple and that there was no reason why their intimacy should be interrupted.

It was therefore agreed eight days before the fête, that Landry should remain at La Priche and Sylvinet with his parents; for he had become more reasonable, and Barbeau being frequently laid up with the fever, he was of great service on the farm. Sylvinet had a dread of being sent away from home, and this dread had exercised a salutary influence over him, by inciting him to conquer the excess of his affection for Landry, or, at least, to conceal it from others. Peace and happiness had therefore returned to La Bessonnière, though the twins saw each other but once or twice during the week. The fête of St. John was to them a day of happiness and delight. They went together to see the servants hire themselves, and the dance which followed in the marketplace. Landry danced more than one *bourree* with the beautiful Madelon, and to please his brother Sylvinet tried to dance also, but he did not succeed very well till Madelon, taking him as their *vis-a-vis*, kindly showed him the steps, upon which he promised to learn dancing, that he might partake of a pleasure where hitherto he had often interfered with Landry's enjoyment. As yet Madelon was not an object of Sylvinet's jealousy, perhaps because Landry was still reserved in his manner towards her, and she flattered and encouraged Sylvinet. Being unembarrassed in her intercourse with him, a looker-on might have supposed that of the two it was he

5

whom she preferred. Had not Landry by nature been free from all jealousy, he might perhaps have misunderstood their relative positions, unless indeed instinct had taught him that Madelon only acted thus to give him pleasure and to procure opportunities of meeting.

Matters went on prosperously for about three months until the day of St. Andoche, the patronal fête of La Cosse, which falls at the end of September.

This day, usually one of enjoyment to our twins in the dances and games held under the big walnut trees of the parish, now brought upon them troubles and perplexities for which neither was prepared.

Caillaud having given permission to Landry to sleep the night before at La Bessonnière, that he might be at the fête in good time in the morning, Landry set out before supper, happy in the thought of surprising his brother, who did not expect him till the morrow. At this season of the year the days begin to shorten and night falls quickly. Landry, who knew not what fear meant in the open daylight, would have been very unlike others of his age and country had he been pleased to find himself alone at night upon the highways, above all in the autumn, the very season when witches and hobgoblins enjoy themselves most, under cover of the fogs which assist to conceal their tricks and sorcery. Landry being accustomed to go out at all hours alone in attendance upon his oxen, had no particular fear on this evening, more than any other, but he walked quickly and sang aloud, as one does when the weather is gloomy, since it is well known that human song has power to scare all creatures of ill omen.

Arrived to the right of the ford of Roulettes, so called from certain round stones found there in great quantities, he carefully lifted the legs of his trousers, that the water might reach above his ankles, and took good care not to walk straight, as the ford runs in a slanting direction, with deep holes to the right and the left. Landry knew the ford so well that he could scarcely make a mistake. Moreover, from that point was to be seen through the trees, now half despoiled of their leaves, a small light which issued from the window of Mother Fadet, and by looking at the light and walking towards it, there was no chance of mistaking the road. It was so dark under the trees that Landry tried the ford with his stick before venturing in, and was astonished to find the water higher than usual, especially as he heard the noise of the sluices, which had been open for more than an hour. Still, as he distinctly saw the light in Fanchon's window, he determined to proceed; but ere he had taken two steps the water was above his knees, and he drew back, thinking he had been deceived. He tried again, a little higher up and a little lower down, but in both places he found the water still deeper; yet there had been no rain, and the sluices were all open. He was thoroughly perplexed.

CHAPTER X.

I MUST have taken the wrong road, thought Landry, for certainly I see on my right the candle of Fanchon, which ought to be on my left.

He returned up the road as far as the cross and walked around it with his eyes shut, that he might disabuse his senses; and having thoroughly observed the trees and thickets around, he found he was in the right road and returned to the river; but though the ford appeared all right, he dared not advance, since he suddenly saw, almost behind him, the light from the house of Fanchon, which ought to have been in his face. He returned to the bank, and then the light appeared to be in the right place. He took the ford again at another incline, and this time the water was nearly up to his waist. He still persevered, however, thinking that he had encountered some hole, and that he should soon get out of it by making for the light.

But he was obliged to stop, for the hole kept getting deeper and deeper, and he found himself up to his shoulders in water. It was very cold, and he paused a moment to decide which way he would go, for the light appeared to have changed places again, and he now saw it jumping and darting from one bank to another, finally showing a double reflection, as it bounded over the water.

Landry was frightened, and almost lost his presence of mind, for he now saw that it was a will-

o'-the-wisp, and he had often heard it said that
there was nothing more deceptive and mischievous than this light, misleading travellers by entic-
ing them to the deepest and most dangerous parts
of the river, and then leaving them to their fate.
Landry shut his eyes, that he might not see it, and
rapidly retreating, found himself once more upon
the bank. There he threw himself upon the grass
and watched the hobgoblin pursuing its pranks
and follies. Truly, it was a frightful thing to see;
sometimes spinning round and round like a king-
fisher, sometimes disappearing altogether, while
at others it dilated to the size of an ox's head, and
again was scarcely bigger than the eye of a cat.
At times it came towards Landry, and whirled so
quickly around him that he was quite dazzled, till,
finding that it could not induce him to follow, the
hobgoblin darted away to frisk among the rushes,
where it appeared to give vent to its anger and
vexation.

Landry dare not move, for to retrace his steps
was not the way to put the will-o'-the-wisp to
flight, since every one knows that it delights in
following those who run from it, plaguing and
tormenting them till they grow bewildered and
fall into mischief. He was shivering with cold
and terror, when he heard behind him a sweet
young voice singing merrily, and at the same
moment Fanchon, who was gayly preparing to
cross the water, in perfect unconcern at the gambols of the mysterious hobgoblin, stumbled
against Landry as he lay on the ground.

"It is I, Fanchon," said Landry, rising; "don't be afraid. I am not an enemy."

He spoke thus civilly, because he was almost as much afraid of her as of the will-o'-the-wisp. He had heard her singing, and believed that she was making an incantation to the dreaded spirit, which danced and twisted about like a mad thing, as though glad to see her.

"So, my fine twin!" said Fanchon, after a moment's thought, "you speak soothingly to me, because you are half dead with fear; why, your voice trembles in your throat like that of my old grandmother! Come, poor boy, pride is not so great by night as by day, and I will engage you dare not cross the water without me."

"By my faith, I have just come out of it!" said Landry, "and think myself lucky to have escaped drowning. Are you going to venture, Fanchon? Do you not fear to lose the ford?"

"And pray why should I lose it? But I see the cause of your terror," said Fanchon, laughing. "Come, give me your hand, coward; the goblin is not so wicked as you think, and only does harm to those who are afraid of it. I have often seen it, and we know each other of old."

Thereupon, with more strength than Landry would have given her credit for possessing, Fanchon took him by the arm and drew him into the ford, singing as they went. Landry scarcely felt more at ease in the society of the little sorceress than in that of the will-o'-the-wisp. Still, as he preferred seeing the devil in the form of one of his

own species rather than under that of a flame so
saturnine and restless, he offered no resistance
and quickly resumed his self-possession, as he
found that Fanchon conducted him so well that he
walked dry-footed on the stones. But as they
both walked quickly, thus opening a current of
air, they were still followed by the meteor, as it is
called by the schoolmaster of our parts, who pro-
fesses to know a great deal upon these matters,
and who assures people that there is no danger to
be apprehended from it. It may be that Mother
Fadet was equally wise on this subject and had
taught her granddaughter to fear nothing from
these night-fires, or else, from continually seeing
them—for they were of frequent occurrence
around the ford of Roulettes, and it was by mere
chance Landry had not seen one before—the little
girl had perhaps formed her own idea that the
goblin was not wickedly disposed and only intended her good. Feeling Landry tremble all
over as the meteor approached:

"Simpleton!" said she, "that fire does not burn;
and were you only skillful enough to handle it,
you would find that it would not even leave a
mark."

"This is worse than I thought," said Landry to
himself; "a fire which does not burn—every one
knows where that comes from, since God's fire is
made to warm and burn."

But he did not make this thought known to the
little girl, and when at last he found himself safe
and sound on the opposite bank, he was greatly

tempted to leave her where she was and to make
the best of his way to La Bessonnière.   But Landry was not ungrateful, and he would not quit her
without first expressing his thanks.

"This is the second time you have rendered me
a service, Fanchon Fadet," he said to her, "and I
should be a bad fellow indeed, were I not to tell
you that I shall remember it all the days of my
life.   I was almost distracted when you found me
just now; the will-o'-the-wisp had completely bewildered me, and I never could have managed to
cross the ford but for you."

"You might have crossed it without any difficulty, if you had not been so foolish," replied Fanchon; "I would never have believed that a great
fellow like you, in his seventeenth year, with a
beard already sprouting on his chin, could be so
easily frightened.   But I am glad to have seen it."

"And pray, why are you glad, Fanchon Fadet?"

"Because I do not like you," said she, in a contemptuous tone.

"And why do you not like me?"

"Because I do not esteem you—neither you,
your twin, your father nor mother; you are all
proud, just because you are rich, and think people
only do their duty in rendering you a service.
They have taught you to be ungrateful, Landry;
and next to being a coward that is the worst fault
a man can be guilty of."

Landry felt greatly humiliated at these reproaches, for he could not help seeing that they
were not altogether undeserved, and he replied

"If I have been wrong, Fanchon, impute the blame to me only. Not a soul in our house is aware of the assistance you formerly rendered me, but now they shall know all, and you shall have whatever reward you desire."

"There is pride for you!" exclaimed Fanchon. "So you think a present will discharge all obligation! You think I am like my grandmother, who, provided she is well paid, will submit to all sorts of insolence and ill-treatment. But know that I desire none of your gifts; that I despise all that belongs to you, because you have not had the gratitude to speak one word of kindness and thanks during the whole twelvemonth which has passed since I relieved you in your hour of distress."

"I have been wrong, and I confess it, Fanchon," said Landry, who could not help being astonished at the manner in which, for the first time, he heard her reason. "But you have also been somewhat to blame. It did not require much sorcery to help me to find my brother, since you had doubtless seen him while I was talking to your grandmother; had you really possessed a kind heart, you, who reproach me with the hardness of mine, instead of keeping me in suspense and suffering, instead of telling me what might have led me farther astray, you would have said at once, 'Go down to the meadow and on the bank of the river you will find your brother.' This would have cost you but little trouble. Instead of which you destroyed the value of the service you rendered me by playing with my feelings."

Fanchon, quick as she usually was at repartee, hesitated for a moment, then said:

"I see you have done your utmost to banish gratitude from your heart and to persuade yourself that you owe me none, because of the reward I exacted from you. But I tell you once again your heart is hard and wicked, for you have failed to observe that I have not only claimed no recompense, but have refrained from reproaching you with your ingratitude."

"That is true," said Landry, who was good faith personified. "I have been wrong; I know it, and am sorry for it. I ought to have spoken to you. I have intended to do so frequently, but you behaved so haughtily I knew not how to set about it."

"Had you come the day after to speak a friendly word you would not have found me haughty; you would have seen directly that I had no intention of receiving payment and we should have been good friends. Instead of which I have formed a bad opinion of you, and am not at all sure that I ought not to have left you to deal with the will-o'-the-wisp as best you could. Good night, Landry. Go and dry your clothes, and tell your parents, 'but for that little beggar of a Cricket I should have had a good ducking in the river this evening.'"

Thus speaking, Fanchon turned her back upon Landry and walked towards her home, singing to herself. Landry was filled with repentance and grief, not that he was disposed to entertain any

very friendly feeling towards a girl whom he
thought more witty than good, and whose un-
couth manners were displeasing even to those
whom they amused.   But he had a generous nature, and could not endure a wrong upon his conscience.   He therefore ran after Fanchon, and,
taking her by the hand, said:

"Come, Fanchon Fadet, this affair must be settled between us.   You are displeased with me and
I am not very well contented with myself.   You
must tell me what you wish, and to-morrow, without fail, I will bring it."

"I wish never to see you again," replied Fanchon harshly; "and bring what you may, you may
rely upon it, I shall throw it in your face."

"These words are too rough for one who offers
you atonement.   If you will accept no gift, there
is perhaps some other way of rendering you a
service, by which I may show that I am not ill-
disposed towards you.   Come, Fanchon, tell me
what shall I do to satisfy you?"

"You will not ask my pardon, then, and desire
my friendship?" she said, pausing.

"Ask your pardon?   That is a good deal to require," replied Landry, who could not bring himself to conquer his pride sufficiently to ask forgiveness of a girl scarcely respected as one of her
age should be.   "As for your friendship, Fanchon, you are so drolly constituted that I could
not have much faith in it; ask me, therefore, for
something which can be given at once and for-

ever, and which I shall not be obliged to take
back."

"Well," said Fanchon, in a dry, clear voice, "it
shall be as you wish, twin Landry. I have offered you a free pardon, and you will not have it.,
Therefore I now claim your promise, which is to
comply with my demand upon the day I require it
of you. That day will be to-morrow, at the fête
of St. Andoche; and what I require is, that you
shall dance three *bourrees* with me after the first
mass, two *bourrees* after vespers, and again two
bourrees after the angelus, which will make in all
seven; and that, through the whole day, from sun-
rise to sunset, you shall dance with no other girl
or woman. If you do not comply, I shall know
that you possess three very bad qualities—ingratitude, cowardice, and want of honor. Good night.
I shall wait for you to-morrow at the church porch
to open the dance."

And so saying, Fanchon, whom Landry had
followed as far as her home, lifted the latch and
entered so quickly that the door was opened and
closed before the twin could offer a word.

CHAPTER XI.

At first Landry thought Fanchon's request so
ridiculous that he was more inclined to laugh
than to be vexed.

"The girl," thought he, "is more mischievous

than ill-disposed, and more disinterested than I would have given her credit for, for the payment she requires will not ruin my family."

But, upon further reflection, he thought the required discharge of his debt harder than it had at first seemed. The little Fanchon danced very well; he had seen her capering in the fields and woods with the peasant lads, upon which occasions she was wont to conduct herself in so impish a manner that they could scarcely keep up with the measure. But then she was so ugly and badly dressed, even upon Sundays and gala days, that no boy of Landry's age would think of dancing with her, above all, in the presence of a number of people; even the swineherds and younger farm lads scarcely thought her worthy of an invitation, while the belles of the neighborhood disliked to have her among them. Landry, therefore, could not help feeling humiliated at the thought of being tied to such a partner; and when he came to consider that he was already engaged for at least three *bourrees* with the beautiful Madelon, the affront he should be compelled to offer her rendered his situation more perplexing and painful. Cold and hungry, and still fearing that the will-o'-the-wisp might follow in his wake, Landry walked rapidly on, without venturing to look behind him; and, as soon as he reached home, related how he had missed the ford in consequence of the dark night, and with what difficulty he had got out of the water. But, ashamed to confess the terror he had experienced, he mentioned neither the will-o'-the-wisp nor Fanchon. Having dried his clothes Landry went to bed, thinking that it would be time enough on the morrow to torment himself with the consequences of this unlucky adventure. His sleep was broken and confused. More than fifty times over did he dream he saw Fanchon astride of the meteor, in form like a large red cock, holding in one of its claws a horn-lantern, with a lighted candle within, whose rays extended over the meadows. And then, suddenly, Fanchon changed into a cricket the size of a goat, and in the voice of a cricket sang to him a song of which he could make nothing save that the rhyme and meter were constantly the same. He grew dizzy and confused, and the light of the meteor appeared to him so bright and vivid that when he awoke his eyes were dazzled, and he could see nothing but small sparks of black, red, and blue, as though he had been gazing at.the sun or moon. Landry, wearied with his restless night, fell asleep during mass, and so lost every word of an eloquent sermon extolling the graces and virtues of the good Saint Andoche. Upon leaving the church Landry was still so tired and sleepy that Fanchon had almost passed from his thoughts; but there she stood at the door, close to the beautiful Madelon, who lingered in the assurance that Landry would claim her hand for the first dance. But as Landry advanced to speak to her the Cricket stepped forward, saying, with matchless effrontery: "Come, Landry, you invited me, yesterday evening, for the first dance, and I do not intend to let you off."

Landry turned red, and observing that Madelon also blushed with surprise and vexation, he took courage to resist Fanchon.

"I may have promised to dance with you, Cricket," he said to her, "but I was already engaged, and your turn will come next."

"Not so," returned Fanchon boldly. "Your memory plays you false, Landry. You can have no previous engagement, since the promise I now claim stands over from last year, and you only renewed it yesterday evening. If Madelon wishes to dance with you to-day let her take your twin, who is your second self, and one is as good as the other."

"The Cricket is right," said Madelon, proudly, taking Sylvinet by the hand; "since your promise is of so long standing you must, of course, keep it. I would just as soon dance with your brother."

"Oh, yes, it's all the same," said Sylvinet, artlessly; "we four will dance together."

It was necessary to move on, that general attention might not be attracted to the party, and the Cricket began to caper with such pride and agility that never was *bourree* better marked or danced. Had she been pretty and well dressed it would have been a pleasure to see her, for she danced admirably; and there was not a belle present who did not envy her lightness and firmness; but the poor child was so shockingly attired that she looked even worse than usual. Landry, chagrined

and humiliated, not daring to look at Madelon,
fixed his eyes on his partner, and thought her
even more repulsive than in her every day rags.
Fanchon had thought to make herself charming,
and she was simply ridiculous. On her head was
a cap, yellow from age, which, instead of being
close at the sides and back, according to the fashion of the day, was open, so as to display two large
flat ears, while a corner fell on her neck, giving
her the look of her grandmother and causing her
head to appear in contrast with her slender neck,
like a bushel on a small stick. Her petticoat of
stuff was too short by a foot and a half, and having
outgrown the bodice during the last year, her lean
sunburnt arms issued from her sleeves like a couple of spider's legs. She wore, besides, a crimson
apron, an heirloom from her unfortunate mother,
the fashion of which she had never thought of al-
tering, though for the last ten years it had ceased
to be worn by young people. The poor girl was
certainly not a coquette; she lived like a boy, caring nothing for her personal appearance and loving only laughter and fun. Thus in her Sunday
dress she looked like a little old woman and was
an object of general ridicule. Yet her attire was
not the result of poverty, but of avarice in her
grandmother and want of taste in the girl herself.
Sylvinet thought it strange that Landry should
have taken a fancy to ask Fanchon to dance, and
Landry knew not what explanation to offer. He
would gladly have hidden himself in the bowels of
the earth. Madelon was displeased, and with the

exception of Fanchon the faces of the whole party were so long that one would have supposed the troubles of the whole world were upon them.

As soon as the first dance was ended Landry made his escape, that he might indulge his mortification in private; but ere many moments were over Fanchon, escorted by the Grasshopper, who, inasmuch as he wore a peacock's feather and a gilt tassel in his cap, was more independent and quarrelsome than usual, found him out, escorted by a troop of girls younger than herself, since those of her own age avoided her society. When Landry saw her with all this tribe, whom she intended to bring as witnesses in case of his refusal to fulfil his promise, he quietly submitted and led her to the walnut trees, where he would gladly have sought for some out of the way corner wherein they might dance unobserved. Fortunately neither Madelon nor Sylvinet nor any of the neighbors were in that quarter, and Landry desired to profit by the opportunity to fulfil his task and dance the third *bourree* with Fanchon., The only spectators near were strangers, who paid no particular attention.

As soon as Landry had finished he ran to find Madelon, and asked her to partake of refreshments with him under the trees. But she had been dancing with some one who had previously requested the same favor, and she haughtily refused our unfortunate twin. But, observing that Landry retired to a corner with his eyes full of tears—for pride and vexation only added to her beauty—she soon rose from the table and said

6

aloud: "The vespers are ringing; with whom shall I dance afterwards?" and, while speaking, she turned towards Landry, expecting him to exclaim "With me!"

But before he could open his lips others had offered, and Madelon, not deigning to cast on him a look of reproach or regret, repaired to vespers with her new beau.

As soon as the vespers were over Madelon returned to the dance with Pierre Aubardeau, followed by Jean Aladenise and Etienne Alaphilippe, who all three successively led her to dance, for she was too pretty and too well off ever to stand in need of partners. Landry watched her in secret. Fanchon, according to custom, had remained praying in the church long after the rest had finished—some said from devotion, others that she might the better disguise her dealings with the devil.

Landry was greatly disturbed at Madelon's indifference, and at the ease with which she consoled herself for the affront he had been compelled to offer her. For the first time the idea suggested itself to him that she might be somewhat of a coquette, and that at all events she could have no great attachment for him, since she amused herself so well without him.

It is true he knew himself to be in the wrong, at least to all appearance; but she had observed his grief as they stood together under the trees, and she ought to have divined the existence of some secret cause, which he would gladly have found an opportunity to explain. Whereas she had shown no concern and was as gay as a young kid, while his heart was breaking with sorrow.

When Madelon had satisfied her three partners Landry drew near her, desiring to speak to her in secret and to justify himself as best he could; but being just at the age when boys are timid and awkward with women, he knew not how to accomplish his object, and finding no word to say, took her gently by the hand to lead her aside. But, instead of complying, Madelon said, with a mixture of anger and kindness:

"So, Landry, you are going to ask me to dance, after all?"

"No, not to dance," he replied (for he was incapable of dissimulating, and no longer thought of breaking his word with Fanchon), "but to tell you something which you cannot refuse to hear."

"Oh, if it be a secret you have to impart, Landry, any other time will do as well," replied Madelon, withdrawing her hand. "This is a day for dancing and fun. I am not yet tired, but since the Cricket has tired you out, you can go home to bed if you will. I shall remain a little longer." So saying, she accepted the offer of Germain Audoux, who came to ask her to dance; and as she turned her back on Landry, he heard Germain Audoux say: "That boy appeared to think this *bourree* was his."

"Perhaps," said Madelon with a toss of the head, "but if so he will find himself disappointed."

Landry was greatly annoyed at these words and

remained near the dancers, that he might observe
Madelon, whose haughtiness and indifference
sadly vexed him; and as he stood watching her
with an expression of careless irony she said,
tauntingly: "Well, Landry, so you cannot find a
partner to-day.   You will be obliged to return to
the Cricket."

"With all my heart," replied Landry; "for if she
be not the belle of the fête, she is certainly the
best dancer."

And forthwith he went to seek Fanchon, and
taking his place directly opposite Madelon, danced
two *bourrees* with her without quitting the spot.
Who shall describe the pride and content of the
Cricket?   Making no effort to conceal her happiness, her roguish black eyes sparkled, while she
held her head with its strange cap erect, like a
tufted chicken.   But unfortunately this triumph
offended five or six lads who were usually her
partners, and who, finding themselves slighted on
the present occasion, began to criticise her dancing, accusing her of pride, and whispering around
her: "See, the Cricket thinks to charm Landry
Barbeau!" coupling her name with sarcasms and
reproaches suggested by anger.

CHAPTER XII.

WHENEVER Fanchon happened to pass near them they would pull her by the sleeve and put out their feet to trip her up, and at last some of the youngest and rudest among them pulled her cap first on one side and then on the other, crying: "Look at the big cap, the big cap of Mother Fadet!"

The poor Cricket dealt a few blows right and left, but this only served to draw attention to her, and caused the bystanders to remark:

"Look at our Cricket, what luck she is in to-day, to dance so many times with Landry Barbeau. It is true she dances well, but see how she plays the fine lady, strutting about like a magpie."

While to Landry some said: "She must have thrown a charm over you, poor fellow, since you can look at no one else, or perhaps you are going to turn sorcerer yourself, and we shall soon see you leading a flock of wolves to the field."

Landry was mortified at these remarks, and Sylvinet, who thought nothing too good for his brother, was still more mortified to find him a laughing-stock for so many people, and, among others, for strangers, who now began to mingle with the crowd, asking questions and saying: "He is a handsome lad; but it is a droll idea to single out the ugliest girl in the whole assembly for his partner."

Madelon, too, with an air of triumph, stood by and listened to these railleries, pitilessly adding her word:

"What could you expect?" said she. "Landry is still a child, and at his age, provided a partner can be secured, it matters not whether it be a sorceress or a Christian."

Upon this Sylvinet took his brother by the arm, saying in a whisper: "Come, Landry, let us go home, or we shall get into a quarrel, for they are all making fun of you, and the insults offered to Fanchon revert to you. I cannot think what has possessed you to dance with her so often; one would suppose you were seeking to make yourself ridiculous; but give over this amusement, I beg. It is all very well for the Cricket to expose herself to the insults and contempt of the world; she desires nothing better; it is her taste; but it is not so with us. Let us go; we can return after the 'Angelus,' and you can dance with Madelon, who is a much more suitable partner. I always told you you liked dancing too well, and that some day it would lead you into trouble."

Landry followed him a few steps, but soon returned on hearing a loud clamor, when he saw Fanchon deprived of her cap by the blow of a fist, from one of the group of boys, to whose mercy Madelon and the rest of the girls had delivered her over. There stood the poor Cricket with her long black hair hanging down her back, weeping with rage and grief at the ill-treatment, which, this time, at all events, she had done nothing to provoke, unable to recover her cap, which a mischievous boy had carried away on the point of a stick. Landry burned with indignation; his good heart revolted at the injustice, and pursuing the boy, he recovered the cap and stick, giving him at the same time a sound beating. The rest fled at his approach, and taking the Cricket by the hand he returned to her the unfortunate headdress. Landry's vivacity and the alarm of the boys made the lookers-on laugh heartily. They showed a disposition to applaud Landry, but Madelon turned the feeling against him, and several boys of Landry's own age thought proper to raise a laugh at his expense.

Landry had now lost all bashfulness; brave and strong, a feeling of manliness told him that he should best fulfil his duty in not allowing a woman to be ill-treated, were she ugly or beautiful, little or big, whom he had taken as his partner to dance. Perceiving the manner in which those about Madelon were looking at him, he went straight up to them, saying: "Well, sirs, I should like to know what you have to say? If it pleases me to pay attention to this girl, what right have you to take offence? And if you are offended, why do you say so in a whisper? Here I am, to give you any answer you may require. Some one called me a child, but there is not a man among you, nor even a boy of any size, who dares say so to my face. I wait for an answer, and we shall see if any one will molest the girl whom I think proper to dance with."

Sylvinet had not quitted his brother's side, for, though he did not approve of his provoking this quarrel, he held himself ready to support him. There were present some four or five boys taller by a head than our twins; but, when they saw Landry and Sylvinet so resolute, not a word was breathed in reply, while they looked from one to the other as though to ask who felt disposed to measure his strength with Landry. No one offered, and Landry, who still held Fanchon by the hand, said to her: "Put on your cap, Fanchon; we will dance another *bourree*, that I may see who will dare to take it from you again."

"No," she said, wiping her tears, "I have danced enough for to-day, and I hold you excused from your promise."

"Not so; you must dance again," said Landry, who was all on fire with courage and pride. "It shall never be said that you cannot dance with me without being insulted."

So saying Landry led her out to dance, and not a word or look of insult was addressed to her. Madelon and her admirers had gone to dance elsewhere, and at the close of the *bourree*, Fanchon whispered to Landry: "It is enough, Landry. You have satisfied me entirely, and I relinquish all claim upon you. I am going home, and you may dance with whom you please for the rest of the evening."

Having thus spoken, Fanchon rejoined her little brother, who was quarrelling and fighting with a group of urchins, and departed so quickly that

Landry could not even see which way she went. The twin then returned home to supper, and as Sylvinet was greatly vexed at all which had taken place, Landry told him of his adventure with the will-o'-the-wisp the evening before; and how Fanchon, having rescued him from danger, whether by magic or simple courage he knew not, had asked as her reward to dance with him seven times at the fête of St. Andoche. Here Landry paused in his relation, being unwilling to let Sylvinet know of his alarm the year before lest he should find him drowned; and in this he was right, for the wicked thoughts which sometimes enter children's heads are only fostered and strengthened by the attention paid to him.

Sylvinet approved of his brother for keeping his word, and told him that the annoyance he had experienced in consequence only increased the esteem he bore him. But alarmed as he was at the thought of the danger Landry had run in the river, he failed to experience anything like gratitude towards Fanchon, for whom his dislike was so strong that he was unwilling to believe either that she had found his brother by chance, or that she assisted him from a kind motive.

"It was she," said he, "who conjured the will-o'-the-wisp on purpose to disturb your mind and cause you to be drowned, but God would not allow it, since you have never sinned mortally. Then this wicked Cricket, taking advantage of your good nature and gratitude, induced you to make a promise, which she knew would be painful and irksome to you to keep. The girl is thoroughly wicked, all sorcerers love evil, and cannot, if they would, be good. She knew she would produce a misunderstanding between you and Madelon and estrange your best friends. She also intended to make you fight, and if for the second time God had not defended you against her wicked tricks, you would have got into some serious quarrel, which in all probability would have ended in mischief."

Landry, who willingly saw through the eyes of his brother, thought he might perhaps be right, and did not defend Fanchon against his suspicions. They then talked together concerning the goblin, which Sylvinet had never seen, but of which he was curious to hear, though without the slightest desire of encountering it. But they took care not to speak on the subject to their mother, who was afraid even to think of it; nor to their father, because he always laughed at such tales, and had seen the meteor twenty times without disturbing himself about it.

The dancing was to be kept up till midnight, but Landry, whose heart was sad, inasmuch as he had broken forever with Madelon, felt no desire to avail himself of the liberty Fanchon had restored him; he therefore assisted his brother to drive in the cattle from the pastures, and as this took him half way to La Priche and his head ached, he wished Sylvinet good night on the spot, promising to avoid the ford of Roulettes, lest the Cricket or the goblin might play him another trick. Instead, therefore, of crossing by the meadows, he made for the little bridge at the mill, and as the air was still filled with the sound of revelries, he went on his way in peace, well knowing that spirits practise their arts only when the world is asleep. Arrived at the bottom of the hill, he heard to the right of the quarry a sound like some one weeping and crying, which at first he took to be the note of the curlew. But as he drew nearer human sobs became audible, and as his heart never failed him when he had to deal with beings of his own species, especially when they needed assistance, he boldly descended the quarry. At the sound of footsteps the person, whoever it was, became silent.

"Who is it weeping?" said Landry in a firm voice. Not a word came in reply.

"Is any one ill here?" he asked again.

And as still no reply came, he thought of departing, but first looking among the stones and thistles which encumbered the spot, he saw, by the light of the moon, some one lying full length on the ground, motionless, and with the face downward, as though dead. Landry had never yet seen a corpse, and the idea that this might be one caused him great emotion; but he overcame the feeling, and thinking it his duty to assist his neighbor he resolutely approached, and touched the hand of the extended person, who finding discovery unavoidable, half rose, and disclosed to the astonished Landry his partner of the day, Fanchon.

CHAPTER XIII.

LANDRY was at first vexed to find Fanchon thus constantly crossing his path, but as she appeared to be in trouble, he took compassion upon her, and the following conversation passed between them:

"Why, Cricket, is it you who are crying so bitterly? Has any one molested you anew, that you weep thus, and have come hither to conceal yourself?"

"No, Landry; no one has interfered with me since you so bravely defended me; besides, I fear nothing. I hid myself on purpose to cry, for there is nothing so foolish as to expose one's sorrow to indifferent persons."

"But why are you so greatly distressed? Is it because of the tricks played upon you to-day? You were not altogether free from blame yourself, but I must try and console you instead of remonstrating with you further."

"What makes you say, Landry, that I was to blame? Was my wish to dance with you an offence? And why am I the only girl who has not the right to amuse herself like others of her age?"

"It is not that, Fanchon. I do not reproach you for having wished to dance with me. I complied with that wish, and I hope I acquitted myself toward you as I ought. Your fault, if you have committed one, is of older date than to-day,

and is not against me, but against yourself, as you
must well know."

"No, Landry, as true as there is a heaven above
us, I do not know what fault you mean. I have
never given a thought to myself, and if now I see
cause for reproach, it is for having been the unin-
tentional source of vexation and annoyance to
you."

"Do not heed me, Fanchon; I have no complaint to make. Let us speak of yourself, and
since you are unconscious of your faults, will you
allow me, in good faith and friendship, to tell you
what they are?"

"Certainly, Landry, and I shall esteem your so
doing at once the best reward and the best punishment you can give me for the good and the ill I
have caused you."

"Well, then, Fanchon Fadet, since you speak
so reasonably, and I find you for the first time in
your life disposed to be gentle and tractable, I will
tell you frankly why you are not respected as a
girl of sixteen has a right to be. It is because you
are unlike all other girls of your age; your manners and appearance are those of a boy; you take
no care of your person; you are never clean and
neat; and you make yourself ugly and disagreeable by your bad dress and language. You know
well the children often call you by a name still
more displeasing than that of Cricket. Now, tell
me; is it right, at sixteen, to be more like a boy
than a girl? You climb trees like a cat, and will
even jump on a horse without saddle or bridle

and ride like one possessed. It is good to be
strong and active, it is also good to be devoid of
fear; these are excellent qualities for a man, but
for a woman, if she displays them too much, people are apt to accuse her of wishing to make herself conspicuous. Thus, you are criticised, quar-
relled with, hallooed after like a wolf. You are
quick-witted, and your replies to impertinences
provoke lookers-on to laugh; but, while again it is
good to have more wit than the rest of the world,
one is apt to make enemies by constantly using it.
You are inquisitive, and when you have discovered the secrets of another, you throw them in his
teeth upon the first occasion of displeasure he
gives you. This causes you to be feared, and
what we fear we detest. In short, whether you
be a sorceress or not, you seek to be thought one,
that you may have it in your power to terrify
those who displease you, and this is surely a very
bad reputation to rejoice in. These are your
faults, Fanchon Fadet, and it is on account of
these faults that people ill treat you. Reflect on
what I say, and you will see that if you would only
be more like others they would soon learn to value
the real superiority of your mind."

"Thank you, Landry," replied Fanchon, with a
grave and serious air. "The faults others upbraid
me with you have just told me of frankly and
kindly, and if you wish to hear what I have to say
in reply you must seat yourself by my side for a
moment."

"The place is not very suitable," said Landry,

who had no desire to remain long, at this late hour, with a reputed sorceress, and whose thoughts were occupied with the evil charms his companion was accused of throwing around the unguarded.

"All places will be alike unsuitable to you," replied the Cricket, "for the rich are difficult to please. They must have fine grass to sit down on out of doors, and their meadows and gardens afford the most lovely places and the most delicious shade. But the poor do not exact so much from the good God, and are content to lay their heads on the nearest stone. The thorns have no wounds for their feet, and be they where they may, they recognize that all is fitting and beautiful in heaven and upon earth. Nothing is bad, Landry, to those who know the virtue of all things God has created. For myself, without witchcraft, I know the use of the smallest herb we crush beneath our feet; and, knowing its use, I despise neither its odor nor appearance. I say this to you, Landry, that I may presently teach you something which relates to Christian souls, no less than to the flowers of the garden and the brambles of the highway. People too often despise those things which appear neither beautiful nor good, and in so doing deprive themselves of what is valuable and useful."

"I do not altogether understand what you mean," said Landry, seating himself by her side; and for a moment they remained silent, for the mind of Fanchon was wrapt in thoughts of which Landry knew nothing, while he, in spite of headache and fatigue, could not avoid a certain feeling of pleasure as he listened to her words. Never had he heard a voice so gentle, and words so full of wisdom as the voice and words of Fanchon at that moment.

"Listen, Landry," she continued; "I am more to be pitied than blamed, for if guilty of wrongs towards myself, at least I have never committed any serious wrong towards another, and were people just and reasonable, they would think more of my good heart than of my ugly face and shabby clothes. Reflect a moment, or learn, if you do not already know it, what my fate has been since I came into the world. I shall speak no ill of my poor mother, whom every one, in her absence, blames and insults, while I cannot undertake to defend her, since I scarcely know the wrong she has committed, or why she was driven to do it; yet the world is so wicked that while I still wept for the loss of my mother I was taunted and reproached for her fault, and my own shamelessness in not blushing for it. In my place, perhaps, as you say, a sensible girl would have sought refuge in silence, deeming it prudent to abandon the cause of her mother, that she might herself escape; but I could not do this; my affection was stronger than my prudence; my mother was still my mother; and, let her have done what she may, let me find her again or never hear her spoken of more, I must ever love her with all the strength of my heart. Feeling thus, when they call me the child of the *vivandiere*, I am angry—not for my-

self, but for my unfortunate mother, whom it is
my duty to defend; and, not knowing how to do
that, I avenge her by telling to others the truths
they deserve to hear, by showing them that they
are not more worthy than she whom they calum-
niate.   This is why they call me curious and inso-
lent, and say that I surprise their secrets on purpose to disclose them.   And it is true that the
good God has made me curious, if it be curiosity
which leads me to covet the knowledge of hidden
things.   Had people been kind and humane towards me I should never have thought of satisfy-
ing that curiosity at the expense of my neighbor;
it would have been confined to the knowledge of
such secrets as my grandmother teaches me for
the cure of the human body.   Flowers, herbs,
stones—these would have furnished me with oc-
cupation and amusement, for I love dearly to pen-
etrate into the mysteries of such things—to wan-
der in unfrequented spots and meditate on a thousand things which I never hear mentioned by
people who think themselves wise and clever.
When I allow myself to be drawn into communica-
tion with my neighbors, it is from a desire to render them service with the little knowledge I have
gained, and by which my grandmother herself
often profits, without acknowledging it.   And
then, instead of receiving the thanks of the children whose wounds and diseases I have cured,
and to whom I impart my remedies without
thought of recompense, I am treated as a sorceress, and those who come begging to me meekly

7

enough afterwards assail me with the vilest insults. This, I confess, has often enraged me, and
I might easily have done them an injury in return; for if I know what will do good, I know also
what will do harm; and yet I have never used that
knowledge to their hurt, avenging myself in
words, saying what came to my tongue, and then
forgiving and forgetting, as God has commanded.
As for taking no care of my person or appearance,
that ought to show that I am not foolish enough
to think myself handsome, when I am in fact so
ugly no one can bear to look at me twice. I have
been told this often enough to make me know it,
and, seeing how cruel and contemptuous people
are towards the ugly and poor, I take pleasure in
annoying and vexing them, consoling myself in
the thought that my face is not repulsive to God,
and that my guardian angel will never reproach
me with it. So you see I am not one of those
who say, 'Look at this caterpillar; what an ugly
brute! it must be killed!' I do not crush the poor
creature of a good God; and if the caterpillar falls
into the water I hold out a leaf to save it. And
thus I have earned for myself the reputation of
loving evil beasts, and of being a sorceress, because I do not like to see a frog suffer, the legs of
a wasp pulled off, or a bat nailed alive against a
tree. 'Poor things,' I say to them, 'if every ugly
thing ought to be killed, I have no right to live
any more than you.'"

Landry was greatly touched at the humble and
tranquil manner in which Fanchon spoke of her

ugliness, and remembering her features, which it
was now too dark to see, he replied, without any
thought of flattery:

"But, Fanchon, you are not so ugly as you
think fit to say. Many girls are plainer than you
who yet never meet with reproach."

"It matters not that I am more or less ugly, Landry, since you cannot call me pretty. But do not
seek to console me, for I have no regrets on that
score."

"But who can tell how you would look, if you
dressed like other people, and wore your hair in a
different fashion? One thing everybody says,
and that is that if your nose were not so short,
your mouth so large, or your skin so black, you
would not be at all ill-looking; and they also say
that in the whole country round there is not such
another pair of eyes as yours, and that, were they
less bold and mocking in expression, many a lad
would like to be favorably regarded by them."

Landry spoke without taking much heed to
what he was saying, feeling for the first time an interest in Fanchon which a few moments before he
would have believed impossible. This did not
escape her observation, but she was too wise to
attach much value to it.

"Mine are eyes which see with pleasure what is
good," said she, "and with pity what is not. Thus
I easily console myself for displeasing those who
do not please me, and few things puzzle me more
than to see the belles of the village coquetting
with every admirer, as though each one among

them was to their taste.   Now, for my part, were
I handsome, I should not care to appear so, or to
render myself agreeable, save to those who
pleased me."

At these words Landry's thoughts flew to Madelon, but Fanchon gave him little time for such
reflection, and continued to speak as follows:

"In this, then, Landry, consists the full extent of
my wrong-doing to others, that I seek neither
pity nor indulgence for my ugliness, and that I
show myself as I am, without any attempt at disguise, and in the offence thus given people forget
that I have often done them good, and never evil.
But suppose I were inclined to care for my personal appearance, where should I find the means
for ornaments and finery?   Though I have not a
halfpenny in the world I am no beggar, and as for
my grandmother, she hardly gives me food and
lodging.   Is it my fault if I do not know how to
make the most of the poor things left me by my
mother, since no one has taught me, and since,
from the age of ten, I have been abandoned, un-
loved and uncared for?   I know well the nature of
the reproaches lavished upon me, and which
you have been charitable enough to spare me.
People say that, being sixteen years old, I could
hire myself out and so earn the means for my own
maintenance, adding that it is my love of an idle
and vagabond life which keeps me with my grandmother, who bears me no love, and who could
well afford to keep a servant if she would."

"And is not this true, Fanchon?" asked Landry.

"You are accused of disliking work, and your grandmother herself says to all who will listen to her complaints, that she should gain by taking a servant in your place."

"My grandmother says so because she loves to grumble and complain, and yet when I speak of quitting her, she detains me, well knowing that I am of more use to her than she cares to admit. She has no longer the eyes and legs of fifteen with which to seek herbs for her drinks and powders, and some of them are to be found only in far-off and difficult places. Besides, as I have always told you, I myself find properties in herbs with which she is unacquainted, and sometimes, to her great surprise, produce a drug, whose beneficial effects she cannot deny. As for our live stock, they are all so handsome and healthy that people are surprised to find such a herd reared on no better pasture than the common. Well, my grandmother knows to whom she is indebted for sheep with such fine wool, and goats with such good milk, and, believe me, she has no desire that I should leave her, for I am worth more to her than I cost. Spite of the privations and ill tempers to which my grandmother subjects me, I cannot help loving her; and then I have another reason for remaining with her, which I will tell you, Landry, if you please."

"Pray do," replied Landry, who was not at all tired of listening.

"It is," said she, "for the sake of a poor child, whom my mother left to my care when I was only

ten years of age, as ugly as myself, only deformed,
lame from his birth, sickly, crooked and always in
trouble or mischief.   My poor little Grasshopper,
how every one torments and teases him!   Even
my grandmother, were I not by to defend him,
would scold him too roughly and strike him too
hard.   Sometimes I pretend to chastise him myself, but you may be sure I take care not to touch
him in reality, and he knows this, poor little fellow, and when he has done wrong he runs to hide
himself behind my petticoats, crying, 'Beat me
before my grandmother can catch me,' and then I
pretend to beat him and the cunning child affects
to cry. l do my best to take care of him.   I cannot always prevent his being in rags, but whenever I get anything I make it up into clothes for
him, and when he is ill I nurse and cure him;
whereas my grandmother would be the cause of
his death, for she knows nothing of children.   In
short, I preserve the life of this poor little sufferer,
for without me he would be utterly miserable, and
would soon lie in the grave by the side of our
father, whose life I was unable to save.   I know
not whether I am rendering him a real service by
keeping him alive, deformed and ugly as he is, but
I cannot do other, Landry, and when I think of
taking service that I may earn some money and
escape from my miserable existence, my heart
melts with pity and reproaches me as though I
were the mother of the Grasshopper, and as
though I were about to doom him to death.   Such

are my faults and failings, Landry. May the good God be merciful to me, as I forgive all who wrong and misjudge me."

———

CHAPTER XIV.

LANDRY listened to Fanchon with great attention, but could find nothing to oppose in her arguments. The affectionate manner in which she spoke of her little brother, the Grasshopper, as he was called, produced a sudden feeling of friendship for her, and a desire, as it were, to espouse her cause against all the world.

"For once, Fanchon," said he, "any person who would contradict you would be in the wrong himself; all you have just said is good and true, and no one can doubt your excellent heart and sound sense. Why do you not always appear as you are? People then would cease to speak ill of you, and some few would render you justice."

"I have told you already, Landry, that I do not wish to please those who do not please me," replied Fanchon.

"Then you speak thus to me, because"—and here Landry paused, amazed at what he had been about to say, then continued:

"Is it because you have more esteem for me than for any one else? But I thought you hated me, because I have never been kind to you."

"It is just possible I may once have hated you,"

returned Fanchon; "but if it has been so, it is so
no more from to-day, and I will tell you why. I
thought you proud, and so you are; but you know
how to overcome your pride in the performance
of a duty, and this increases your merit. I thought
you ungrateful, but although the pride which has
been instilled into you almost rendered you so,
you are so faithful to your word that nothing
could induce you to swerve from it. I thought
you cowardly, and for that again I was tempted to
despise you; but I find you are only superstitious,
and that want of courage when there is a tangible
danger to confront is not among your faults. You
danced with me to-day though it mortified you
greatly to do so. You even came after vespers to
seek me at the church, when, having said my
prayers, I had forgiven you in my heart, and
thought no longer of tormenting you. You defended me against wicked boys, and challenged
the big ones, who, but for you, would have ill-
treated me. And now, this evening, hearing me
cry, you came to assist and console me. Do not
suppose, Landry, that I can ever forget these
things. All your life long you shall receive proofs
that I preserve a grateful remembrance of them,
and whenever you require a service at my hands
you have only to ask. And now, to begin. I
know I have been the cause of a great sorrow to
you this very day. I am sorceress enough to
divine that, though this morning I had no such
suspicion. Believe me, I am more mischievous
than wicked, and had I known you were in love

with Madelon nothing could have induced me to compromise you with her, as I did by requiring you to dance with me. It amused me to see you quitting the side of a beautiful girl to dance with an ugly one like myself; but I thought it only a mortification to your pride. When I discovered by degrees that the wound was in your heart, that, spite of yourself, you could not keep your eyes from Madelon, and that her displeasure almost made you weep, I could not help weeping myself. I wept when you would have fought with her admirers, and the tears which you mistook for tears of anger were indeed tears of remorse. This is why I was still crying so bitterly when you surprised me here, and why I shall continue to cry till I have atoned for the mischief I have brought on a good and brave lad, as I now know you to be."

"And supposing you were the cause of trouble between me and the girl I love, as you say, how can you produce a good understanding between us?" asked Landry, troubled at the sight of the tears which flowed afresh down the cheeks of Fanchon.

"Leave that to me, Landry," she returned. "I am not so silly but I can express myself as I wish. Madelon shall know that the fault is all on my side; I will tell her everything, and wash you white as snow from all blame. If you are not forgiven to-morrow, it will be because she never really loved you, and"——

"And so I ought not to regret her, Fanchon; but

as, in fact, she never loved me, you will only give
yourself useless trouble; do not, therefore, make
the attempt; and think no more of the slight uneasiness you have caused me; it has already passed
away."

"Such sorrows are not so easily forgotten," returned Fanchon, impetuously; then checking herself, she added, "at least they say so. Your indignation makes you speak thus, Landry; when you
have slept upon it, and to-morrow is come, you
will be very unhappy till you have made your
peace with the beautiful girl."

"Perhaps so," said Landry; "but just now, I
give you my word, I care nothing about it. It
appears to me that you wish to persuade me I am
seriously attached to Madelon, while if ever I did
entertain any affection for her it was so slight that
I have already lost all recollection of it."

"This is singular," said Fanchon, with a sigh;
"is this how you boys love, then?"

"And pray, do you girls love any better, when
you are so easily offended and so readily console
yourselves with the first comer? But we are
speaking of things which, perhaps, we do not as
yet understand, at least you, Fanchon Fadet, who
are always laughing at lovers. I believe you are
amusing yourself at my expense even now, when
you desire to effect a reconciliation with Madelon. Pray do not attempt it, for she may believe
you are commissioned by me, and that thought
would greatly deceive her. Besides, she may be
vexed at the idea of my presenting myself before

her as her chosen lover, when in fact I have never
addressed a word of love to her, and though I
liked to be near her and to dance with her, she
never gave me any encouragement to say so in
words. Let the matter take its own course; she
may think better of it if she pleases, and if not,
why I do not think it will kill me."

"I know better what you think and feel, Landry, than you know yourself," returned Fanchon.
"I believe you when you tell me you have never
made known your attachment to Madelon in
words, but she must be very stupid not to have
gathered it from your eyes, especially to-day.
Since I have been the cause of your sorrow, I
must also be the cause of your joy, and this is a
good opportunity to let Madelon know that you
love her. I will undertake it, and I will manage
matters so delicately and skillfully that she shall
never be able to accuse you of having sent me.
Trust Fanchon, Landry, the poor ugly Cricket,
who is not so ugly within as without, and forgive
her for having tormented you, for the great good
which shall result to you therefrom. You shall
learn that if it be sweet to possess the love of a
beautiful girl, it is also useful to possess the friendship of an ugly one, for ugly girls are disinterested
and do not easily take offence."

"Whether you be ugly or beautiful, Fanchon,"
said Landry, taking her hand, "I think I can understand that your friendship is an excellent
thing; so excellent that love may be bad in com-
parison. I know now that you possess real good-

ness, for I have offered you to-day a great affront of which you have taken no notice, and while you say I conducted myself well towards you, I feel I have behaved very rudely."

"But how, Landry? I know not in what"——

"In that I did not once kiss you after the dance, Fanchon, when, according to custom, it was both my duty and my right. I treated you as we treat little girls of ten years old, whom we do not condescend to embrace, and yet you are almost my own age; there is not more than a year's difference. I therefore offered you an insult, and were you not so good a girl you would have quickly perceived it."

"I have not even thought of it," said Fanchon, rising, for she felt she was not speaking the truth, and did not wish it to be known.

"Stay," said she, forcing herself to appear gay, "listen how the crickets are singing in the corn-field; they call me by name, and the owl below announces to me the hour, while the stars mark the dial of the heavens."

"I hear them too, and I must also return to La Priche, but before I say adieu, Fanchon, will you not forgive me?"

"I have nothing to pardon, Landry."

"Yes, yes," said Landry, who had become strangely agitated while she was speaking of love and friendship in a voice so soft that the warbling of the bull-finches as they slept upon the bushes appeared harsh after it. "Yes, yes, you owe me forgiveness, that is to say, I must kiss you now to repair the omission of to-day."

Fanchon trembled slightly; then, recovering her self-possession:

"You wish, Landry, that I should make you expiate your fault by a punishment? Well, I will excuse you, my brave boy. It is quite enough to have danced with the ugliest of the party; it would require too great an effort of virtue to kiss her."

"Stay, do not say that," said Landry, taking her hand and arm at the same time; "I think it cannot be a punishment to kiss you, unless, indeed, it is repugnant and distasteful to you, as coming from me."

And when he had said this, he desired so greatly to kiss Fanchon that he trembled for fear lest she should not consent.

"Listen, Landry," said she, in her soft and soothing voice; "were I handsome I should tell you that this is neither the place nor the hour to kiss, as it were in secret. Were I a coquette I should think, on the contrary, that it is both the hour and the place, since night conceals my ugliness, and there is no one here to make you ashamed of your fancy. But, as I am neither handsome, nor a coquette, this is what I have to say to you. Press my hand in token of sincere friendship, and I shall be happy to possess that friendship, I, who have never known nor desire to know the friendship of any other."

"Yes," said Landry, "I press your hand with all my heart, Fanchon. But the most sincere friendship, that which I entertain for you, does not forbid a kiss. If you deny me this proof I shall think you have still some cause of annoyance with me!"

And Landry tried to kiss her by surprise, but she resisted, and as he persevered began to cry, saying: "Leave me, Landry, you cause me great grief."

Landry desisted in astonishment, and was so vexed to see her still in tears that he was almost angry.

"I see," said he, "that you do not speak the truth when you tell me that my friendship is the only friendship you desire to possess. You have some stronger affection which forbids you allowing me to kiss you."

"No, Landry," replied she, sobbing; "but I fear that for having kissed me at night when you cannot see me you will hate me when you see me in the day."

"Have I never seen you, then?" said Landry, impatiently; "do I not see you now? Stay, come more into the light of the moon. Now I see you clearly. I know not if you be ugly, but I like your face because I like you;" and so saying, he kissed her; first timidly, but at last with such fervor that she grew alarmed, and repulsing him, said: "Enough, Landry, enough; you kiss me as though you were in a rage, or as though you were thinking of Madelon. Be quiet; I will speak to her to-morrow, and to-morrow you shall kiss her with more pleasure than I can give you."

Thus saying, she quickly disappeared from his sight. Landry had a great inclination to run after her, and it was some time before he could determine to pursue his own road. At last, fearing that he was bewitched, he also began to run, and did not stop till he reached La Priche.

On the morrow, at break of day, he went to look after his oxen, and while feeding and caressing them, he reflected seriously on the long hour's talk he had had the evening before with Fanchon, and which had appeared to him but a moment. His head was still confused with sleep, and the fatigue of a day so different from what he had expected; he felt troubled and bewildered at the feelings he had experienced for this girl, who now appeared to him ugly and ill-dressed, as he had always known her. For some moments he imagined he must have dreamed of the desire he felt to kiss her, and the happiness it had afforded him to press her to his heart, just as though he entertained a great love for her, and as though she had suddenly appeared to him the most amiable and beautiful girl in the world.

"She must be a witch, as they say, though she denies it," thought he; "for certainly she bewitched me last evening, and never, in the whole course of my life have I felt for father, mother, sister, or brother, not even for the beautiful Madelon, nor for my dear twin Sylvinet, such a transport of affection as, for two or three minutes, this sorceress inspired me with. If my poor Sylvinet could have seen what was passing in my heart he would certainly have been devoured with jealousy. The attachment I had for Madelon did no wrong to my brother, whereas, were I to remain only one day, infatuated as I was for a moment, by the side of this Fanchon, I should go mad and love nothing but her in the whole world."

And Landry felt almost stifled with shame, fatigue, and impatience. He sat down upon the manger of his oxen, dreading lest the sorceress should deprive him of courage, reason and health.

But as the day advanced, the laborers of La Priche made their appearance, and began to joke him upon his dance with the ugly Cricket, whom they represented as so ugly, so ill-mannered and badly dressed that Landry knew not where to hide himself from shame, not alone at what his comrades had seen, but at what he took care not to let them know.

He did not, however, lose his temper, for the people of La Priche were his friends and showed no ill feeling in their jests. Landry had even the courage to tell them that Fanchon was not what they thought, that she was better than many others of good repute, and that she was capable of rendering excellent service to those who dealt fairly by her. Upon this they rallied him still more.

"Her grandmother may be skillful," said they, "but as for Fanchon, she is an ignorant child, and if you have a sick beast I advise you not to follow her prescriptions, for she knows not a single medicinal secret. She knows how to bewitch boys, though, it appears, Landry, since you scarcely quitted her side yesterday. You will do well to take care, my poor fellow, or you will soon be called Cricket and Grasshopper yourself. The devil will be after you, and we shall be obliged to get your exorcised."

"I believe," said the little Solange, "that he must have put his stocking on wrong side out yesterday morning, for that always attracts sorcerers, and Fanchon must have seen it."

CHAPTER XV.

DURING the day Landry, being occupied with his work, saw Fanchon pass by. She was walking quickly towards a copse where Madelon was grazing her sheep. It was the hour for unyoking the oxen, half the day's labor being accomplished, and Landry, while taking them to pasture, still watched Fanchon running along, with a step so light that the grass beneath her feet was scarcely seen to bend. He was curious to know what she would say to Madelon, and instead of hastening to eat his soup, which was waiting for him in the furrow, yet warm from the ploughshare, he crept gently by the side of the copse to listen to what these two young girls would say to each other. He could not see them, and, as Madelon murmured her replies in a low voice, he was unable to hear what she said, but the voice of Fanchon, though soft, was very clear, and he lost not a word, though she also conversed in a low tone. She spoke of him to Madelon, and told her, as she had promised, of the pledge which she had exacted from him ten months before, to be at her command whenever she should require his services. And this she explained so sweetly and humbly that it was a pleasure to listen to her, and then, without mentioning the will-o'-the-wisp or Landry's terror, she told how he had been almost drowned by missing the ford of Roulettes on the eve of St. Andoche. In short, she showed to his advantage all that had occurred and insisted that the mischief had arisen from the vanity which had prompted her to desire to dance with a big boy, when before she had danced only with little ones.

Upon this Madelon raised her voice as in anger and said: "What is all this to me? You may dance your whole life with the twins if you will, but do not believe, Cricket, that it will vex or annoy me for a moment."

"Do not speak so harshly concerning poor Landry, Madelon, for he has given you his heart, and if you will not accept it he will be more grieved than I can tell you."

And then she went on to represent this grief in such pretty language and in so caressing a tone, awarding such praise to Landry, that he blushed with pleasure to hear himself so extolled.

Madelon was astonished to hear Fanchon

speak so well, but her contempt was too great to
allow her to show this.

"You have a ready, bold tongue," said she,
"and one would suppose your grandmother had
given you a lesson how to cajole people, but I do
not like to talk to sorcerers; it brings misfortune;
so I beg you to leave me, Horned Cricket. You
have found a beau; now keep him; for he is the
first and the last who will ever take a fancy to
your ugly phiz. As for me, I do not covet your
leavings, even were he the son of a king. Your
Landry is but a fool, and can not be worth much,
since, knowing you have seduced him from me,
you already ask me to take him back. A pretty
lover for me, indeed, must he be whom Fanchon
Fadet does not care to retain!"

"If it be that which wounds you," replied Fanchon in a voice which touched Landry's heart to
its depths, "and if you are so proud that you will
not be just till I am humbled, be satisfied, and
trample beneath your feet, beautiful Madelon, the
pride and the courage of the unfortunate Cricket.
You think I disdain Landry, and that were it not
so I should never have asked you to forgive him.
Know, then, since it so pleases you, that I have
loved him for a long while past; that he is the
only one of whom I have ever thought, and it
may be of whom I ever can think, for the rest of
my life; but I am too reasonable and too proud to
believe that I can make him love me in return.
I know what he is, and I know myself. He is
handsome, rich, and respected; I am ugly, poor,

and despised; therefore I know quite well that he is not for me, and you must have seen how he disdained me at the fête. Be then satisfied, since he, to whom Fanchon dare not look up, views you with the eyes of love. Punish the Cricket by despising her and taking back the lover she dare not dispute with you. If not from affection for him, let it be to punish my insolence, and promise me that, when he comes to offer you his excuses you will receive him kindly and forgive him."

Instead of being softened by this submission and devotion, Madelon was hardened, and dismissed Fanchon, still saying that Landry was admirably suited to her, while on her part she thought him too childish and foolish. But the self-sacrifice of Fanchon brought its own reward, in spite of the rebuffs of the beautiful Madelon. The heart of woman is so constituted that a youth appears in the light of a man as soon as he is esteemed and valued by other women. Madelon, who hitherto had never thought seriously of Landry, had no sooner dismissed Fanchon than she began to do so. She reflected on all that beautiful speaker had told her of Landry's love, and, remembering that Fanchon had avowed her own attachment, she rejoiced in the thought of taking vengeance on the poor girl.

She went in the evening to La Priche, from which her house was only a few yards distant, and, under pretence of seeking one of her sheep, which had got mixed in the fields with those of her uncle, she managed to make Landry see her, and by looks encouraged him to approach and speak. Landry quickly perceived this; for, since he had seen so much of Fanchon, he had grown singularly clear-sighted.

"Fanchon is a sorceress," thought he; "she has restored me to the good graces of Madelon, and has done more for me in a conversation of a quarter of an hour than I could have effected in a whole year. She has a wonderful mind, and a heart such as the good God does not often create." And thinking thus he looked at Madelon, but with so listless an air that she withdrew before he could speak to her. His silence did not arise from any feeling of timidity; timidity with Madelon had vanished, he knew not how; but with it had gone also the pleasure he had formerly derived from her society, and all desire to make himself beloved.

Scarcely had Landry supped when he pretended to retire for the night that he might better effect his escape and proceed to the ford of Roulettes. Here he found the will-o'-the-wisp again carrying on its fantastic gambols, and, as he saw it in the distance, Landry thought:

"So much the better; here is the goblin, therefore Fanchon cannot be far away."

He crossed the ford without fear and without making a single false step, and continued as far as the house of Mother Fadet, where he could see no light, nor hear any sound. Everybody was in bed, and he could only hope that the Cricket—

who often went out of an evening after her grandmother and the Grasshopper had fallen asleep—
might be wandering somewhere about, in which
hope he renewed his search, whistling and singing to attract attention, but he encountered only
the badger, which hastily sought refuge among
the stubble, and an owl screeching from the hol-
low of a tree, and was obliged to return home
without having found an opportunity of thanking the good friend who had done him such
service.

The whole week passed without Landry's
being able to see Fanchon, a circumstance which
annoyed and surprised him greatly.

"She will again think me ungrateful, and yet
it is not my fault that I do not see her. I must
have displeased her by kissing her against her
will, and yet I had no idea of offending her."

During this week he reflected more than he
had ever before reflected in his whole life; he
could not see clearly into his own mind, but he
was thoughtful and agitated, and was obliged to
force himself to work; for neither his fine oxen,
nor his glittering plough, nor the rich red earth
moist with the rains of autumn, any longer suf-
ficed for his contemplations or his dreams.

He went to see his brother on the Thursday
evening, and found him full of thought like himself. Sylvinet's character was very different to
Landry's, though at times both were similarly
affected. One would have supposed, now, that
he had divined something was disturbing the

tranquillity of his brother, though he was far
from suspecting the cause. Sylvinet asked Landry if he had made peace with Madelon, and for
the first time, by replying "yes," Landry uttered
a voluntary falsehood. The fact is he had not
said a word to Madelon, thinking that one time
was as good as another. At last Sunday came,
and Landry was among the first to attend mass.
He entered the church before the bells had ceased
ringing, knowing that Fanchon was accustomed
to arrive at that early hour to make long prayers,
for which every one derided her. He saw a young
girl kneeling in the chapel of the Holy Virgin,
who turned her back towards the people and hid
her face in her hands that she might pray undisturbed. It was the posture of Fanchon, but it
was neither her cap nor dress, and Landry went
out again to see if he could find her under the
porch, which with us is called the Raggery, from
the ragged beggars who assemble there during
the services. The rags of Fanchon were the only
rags missing. Mass had ended and the sermon
begun, when, looking again towards the girl
praying so devoutly in the chapel, she raised her
head, and he recognized the Cricket in a dress
and with an air altogether novel. The poor cos-
tume was still there, the stuff petticoat, the red
apron, and the coarse, untrimmed cap, but all had
been washed and remade during the week. Her
dress was longer, and fell modestly to her stock-
ings, which, like her cap, were white as snow.
That singular cap, too, had acquired a new form,

and was now neatly drawn over her black and
smoothly-banded hair. Her neckerchief was
new, and of a pretty, soft yellow, showing her
dark skin to advantage. She had also length-
ened her bodice, and instead of looking like a
piece of dressed wood, her figure was slender and
supple as the body of a beautiful honey-bee.
Moreover, she had washed her hands and face
with some decoction of flowers and herbs till they
were now as soft and sweet as the white thorn of
the spring. Landry, in his surprise at this trans-
formation, let his prayer-book fall, and at the
noise Fanchon turned, and their eyes meeting,
she grew red, but of no deeper shade than the
rose of the thicket, which made her appear almost beautiful, while her black eyes, against
which no one had ever been able to say a word,
were now so clear and brilliant that Landry could
not help thinking:

"She must be a sorceress; ugly as she was, she
wished to be beautiful, and beautiful she is, as by
a miracle."

He was filled with fear, but this fear did not
prevent him from desiring so ardently to speak
with her that, till the end of the mass, his heart
throbbed with impatience.

But Fanchon looked at him no more; and instead of remaining to play with the children when
prayers were over, she departed so quietly that
people had scarcely time to see how changed
and improved she was. Landry dared not follow her, for Sylvinet never took his eyes from

him; but at the end of an hour he succeeded in making his escape, and this time, his heart guiding him aright, he found Fanchon watching her sheep in a small cross-road called the Soldier's Path, because one of the king's soldiers was killed there by the people of La Cosse in olden times, when it was attempted to extort money and service from the peasants exceeding the demands of the law, which were already sufficiently severe.

CHAPTER XVI.

IT being Sunday, Fanchon was neither sewing nor knitting while tending her sheep, but was occupying herself with a quiet amusement which the children of these parts often undertake with considerable interest. She was seeking for four-leaved clover, which is rarely to be met with, and which is said to bring good fortune to the finder.

"Have you found it, Fanchon?" said Landry, as he came up to her.

"Oh, I have often found it," she replied; "but it does not bring happiness with it, as people believe, for it avails me nothing that I have three sprigs of it in my prayer book."

Landry seated himself by her side, as though about to enter into conversation; but a sudden feeling of timidity, more overwhelming than he had ever experienced with Madelon, prevented him from uttering a word.   At this Fanchon

also grew timid; for though the twin said nothing, he looked at her with a singular expression.
At length she ventured to ask him why he appeared so surprised.

"Perhaps," said she, "it is because I have altered my cap. You see I have followed your advice, for I thought that, to appear reasonable, I
must begin by being dressed like other people.
But I have not dared to show myself much this
morning lest I should be reproached with a vain
attempt to render myself less ugly."

"They may say what they like," returned Landry; "for my part I cannot imagine what you
have done to yourself to grow so pretty; for
pretty you now are, and people must shut their
eyes if they do not wish to see it."

"Do not mock me, Landry," replied Fanchon.
"It is said that beauty turns the head of its pos-
sessor, and that ugliness renders one wretched.
I am accustomed to excite terror, and I do not
wish to go mad by believing that I can please.
But it was not on this subject you came to speak
to me, and I would gladly hear that Madelon has
forgiven you."

"I have certainly not come to talk to you of
Madelon. I know not and care not whether she
has forgiven me. But I know you have spoken
to her, and that in such terms that I owe you
many thanks."

"How do you know I have spoken to her? did
she tell you? If so, you must have made your
peace with her."

"We have not made peace, and we do not love each other sufficiently to be at enmity. I know you spoke to her, because she said so to some one who told me."

Fanchon blushed deeply, which made her still more beautiful; for never until that day had her cheeks known that honest color of blended timidity and pleasure which embellishes the plainest. At the same time she was uneasy at the thought that Madelon might have repeated her words, and have made the love she had confessed for Landry a subject for laughter and mirth.

"What has Madelon said of me?" she asked.

"She said I was a great lubber, who could please no girl, not even Fanchon, who shunned and despised me, and who concealed herself all the week that she might not see me, though all the week I was seeking everywhere to find her. I am the laughing-stock of every one, Fanchon, because they know I love you, and you do not love me."

"How false!" cried Fanchon in amazement, for she was not sorceress enough to divine that at the moment Landry was more cunning than herself. "I did not believe that Madelon could be so false and perfidious; but we must forgive her, Landry, for it was vexation which made her speak thus, and that vexation arises from love."

"Perhaps," replied Landry; "and this is why you are not vexed with me, Fanchon; you forgive me everything, because you despise me."

"I do not deserve that you should speak to me

thus, Landry; indeed, indeed, I do not deserve it!
I was never so foolish as to utter the falsehoods
attributed to me.   I spoke quite otherwise to
Madelon, and what I said was for her ear only.
Instead of injuring you in her opinion, it should
have shown her the esteem in which I hold you."

"Listen, Fanchon," said Landry; "do not let us
dispute about what you have or have not said.
You are wise, and I wish to consult you.   Last
Sunday evening I suddenly felt for you, I know
not how, so strong an affection that through the
whole week I have neither eaten nor slept as usual.   I will conceal nothing from you, since, with
so clever a girl, it would be useless.   I confess,
then, that on the Monday morning I was ashamed
of this affection, and would willingly have gone
anywhere to escape falling into such folly again.
But Monday evening I had already so far re-
lapsed that I crossed the ford at night, without
regarding the will-o'-the-wisp, which would willingly have prevented me from seeing you if it
could.   Every morning since I have been almost
frantic at the jokes about my fancy for you, and
every evening I have been almost distracted because I feel that my passion is stronger than my
dread of ridicule.   And now to-day I find you so
pretty, so discreet in your manners and conduct,
that before a fortnight is over, if you continue the
same, not only shall I be forgiven for my love,
but many others will follow my example.   There
will then be no merit in loving you; you will owe
me no preference; and yet, if you will go back to

last Sunday, you cannot but remember that I asked in the evening permission to kiss you, and that I kissed you as ardently as though you had not been considered ugly and disagreeable. These are all the claims I have to offer, Fanchon; tell me if they are acceptable, or if, instead of pleasing, I annoy you."

Fanchon had concealed her face in both her hands, and now made no reply. Landry believed, from what he had overheard of her conversation with Madelon, that he was beloved; and it must be confessed that this knowledge produced such an effect upon him as in some measure to command his love in return. But as he saw the timid and sad attitude of the poor girl, he began to fear that she had only invented a tale to facilitate the reconciliation with Madelon. This thought, while it filled him with grief, served only to increase his passion. He drew her hands from her face; she was as pale as death; and, as he reproached her for her indifference to his love, she fell to the ground, clasping her hands and sobbing, faint, and overcome with emotion. Landry was greatly alarmed, and by rubbing her cold, stiff hands, and holding them in his own, endeavored to restore her. At length she was able to speak, and said:

"I fear you are trifling with me, Landry; and yet there are subjects on which it is cruel to jest. Leave me in peace, I implore you, and never again seek to address me, unless you have some service to ask, when you will always find me ready to aid you."

"Fanchon, Fanchon, it is you who are cruel," said Landry. "It is you who trifle with me. You detest me, and yet you have led me to believe differently."

"I?" said she, in deep affliction; "what can I have led you to believe? I offered, and have given you, an honest friendship, as disinterested as that your brother entertains for you, perhaps more so; for I am not jealous, and, instead of crossing you in your affections, have endeavored to serve you."

"True, true," said Landry; "you have been but too good, and I am wrong to reproach you; forgive me, Fanchon, and let me love you as I can; it may not be so tranquilly as I love my brother, or my sister Nanette; but I promise never to try and kiss you again, since that displeases you."

Landry did, indeed, believe that Fanchon entertained for him only a quiet feeling of friendship, for, being neither vain nor pesumptuous, he was as timid and bashful as though he had not heard, with his own ears, the confession of her love to the beautiful Madelon.

As for Fanchon, she was sufficiently quick-sighted to see that Landry was handsome and madly in love, and it was the overjoy of this discovery which had thrown her into a swoon. But, fearing to lose a happiness so quickly gained, she resolved to test Landry's love by obstacles and time.

He remained with her till night, for, though he dared not renew the subject, he was so fascinated, and took such delight in seeing her and hearing her speak, that he could not resolve to quit her for a moment. He played with the Grasshopper, who, never far from his sister's side, had speedily joined them, and soon discovered that this poor child, so ill-treated and abused, was neither wicked nor mischievous under kind treatment; indeed, before an hour had passed he became so gentle and affectionate that, kissing the hands of the twin, he called him *my* Landry, as he was in the habit of calling his sister *my* Fanchon. Landry soon felt a tender concern for this unfortunate child, and perceived that he, as well as many others, had wronged the poor grandchildren of Mother Fadet, who needed only kindness to render them amiable and agreeable. On the morrow, and several succeeding days, Landry continued to see Fanchon, sometimes in the evening, sometimes in the day, when, unwilling to neglect his duty, he would content himself with an exchange of looks or a few words of greeting warm from his heart. Ere long the improvement in Fanchon's appearance and manners began to attract attention; but, as the opinion of the world is not so easily changed as are our own resolutions, some time had yet to elapse ere she could hope to secure the respect and consideration so long forfeited. Among the gossips of the village were to be found, as is always the case, four or five old men and women who, looking with indulgence upon the follies of youth, constitute themselves, as it were, the parents of all the young people of the neighborhood. Such a party was one evening grouped beneath the walnut trees of La Cosse, and, as they watched the sports around them, the following conversation took place:

"That boy will make a fine soldier by and by if he goes on as he has begun; he has too good a figure to escape service;" such a one "will be as cunning and quick-sighted as his father;" while so-and-so "inherits the wisdom and calmness of his mother." "Young Lucette, there, promises to be a good farm servant, and fat Louise will not lack admirers." "As to our little Marion, give her time and she will be as steady as any."

And when it came to Fanchon's turn to be criticised some one said:

"And what a change has come over the Cricket since the fete of Saint Andoche! She must have been greatly annoyed at the children's rudeness while she was dancing, for she has changed the fashion of her huge cap, and is now no plainer than other girls of her age."

"Have you observed how fair her skin has become of late?" asked Mother Coutourier; "why, her face used to look like a quail's egg, so freckled and sunburnt was it; and the last time I saw her close I was so astonished to find it fair—nay, even pale—that I asked her if she had been ill. Who knows?—many an ugly child has become a handsome girl at sixteen or seventeen."

"And then the older she grows the more reasonable she will become," continued Father Naubin, "and as a girl approaches womanhood she soon learns to render herself pleasing and agreeable. It is high time the Cricket should know she is not a boy. Every one thought she would disgrace the whole neighborhood, but I believe we shall find her no worse than the rest. She will feel bye and bye that she must atone for her mother's bad conduct and, depend upon it, she will give no occasion for scandal herself."

"Heaven grant you may be right," rejoined Mother Courtillet, "for it is too bad for a girl of sixteen to run wild. I am inclined to agree with you about Fanchon, for, when I met her the day before yesterday, instead of mocking my lameness, as usual, she wished me good morning, and asked me how I did, in the civilest manner possible."

"The child is more foolish than wicked," said Father Henri. "I can answer for her good heart, for when my daughter was ill, of her own accord she would take my little grandchildren to play in the fields, and they grew so fond of her that they never cared to leave her."

"Is it true, what people say," asked Mother Coutourier, "that one of Father Barbeau's twins fell in love with her at the last fete of Saint Andoche?"

"You must not believe all you hear," replied Father Naubin. "It was a childish fancy, and the Barbeaus, father, mother and children, are none of them fools."

9

Thus at times did the conversation turn upon Fanchon, though in her continued absence from the village gatherings she was oftener forgotten than remembered.

––––––

CHAPTER XVII.

BUT there was one who saw her frequently, and who paid her the most devoted attention, and that was Landry Barbeau. He would work himself into a frenzy when, by any chance, he was prevented from seeing her. But a few moments in her society were sufficient to restore him to peace and content, so beneficial was her influence upon him. At times the thought would cross his mind that her conduct was not altogether devoid of coquetry; but as her motive was honest, and she simply did not desire his love till he had turned the matter thoroughly over in his own mind, he had no just cause for complaint. On her part she could not doubt the strength of his passion, for it was of a kind not often met with among country people, who love more calmly than the inhabitants of cities. Now Landry was pre-eminently distinguished for patience, and none who knew him well would have dreamed of his allowing himself to be caught so easily; so that Fanchon, seeing how suddenly and entirely he had given himself to her, feared lest the fire so easily kindled might be as rapidly extin-

guished. Though to all appearance Fanchon
had remained a child longer than usual, she possessed good sense and determination far beyond
her years, while her heart was as ardent, perhaps
even more so, than that of Landry. She loved
him to distraction, and yet she conducted herself
towards him with exceeding propriety. Longing
for his presence morning, noon and night, no
sooner had he arrived than she assumed a calm
and tranquil manner; pretending herself to know
nothing of love, that she might the better restrain
his expression. Landry feared nothing so much
as to displease her, and feeling ill-assured of her
love lived with her as though she had been his
sister and he Jeanot, the little Grasshopper.

To distract Landry's attention from thoughts
she was unwilling to encourage Fanchon in-
structed him in all she had acquired herself; initi-
ating him into secrets where her natural talent
had far outrun the lessons of her grandmother,
and as he was still apprehensive of sorcery she
took great pains to make him understand that the
devil had nothing to do with her science.

"Why, Landry," she said to him one day, "you
do nothing but fear the intervention of evil spirits. There is but one spirit, and that is good, for
it is of God. Lucifer is the invention of priests,
as hobgoblins are the inventions of old women.
When I was quite a child I believed in them also,
and was afraid of my grandmother's witchcraft
till she laughed me out of the conceit; for people
are quite right in saying that none believe less in

Satan than the very sorcerers who pretend to invoke him upon every occasion, for they know well that they have never seen or received any assistance from him. My grandmother used to tell me of a certain miller who, taking his cudgel in his hand, set out for four cross roads, to invoke the devil, as he said, and give him a good thrashing; but though he called till he was hoarse the devil never appeared, whereupon the valiant miller returned to his house, boasting ever after that the devil himself was afraid of him."

"But," said Landry, "your belief, my little Fanchon, that the devil has no existence is not very Christian."

"I cannot dispute with you about that," replied she; "but if he exist, I feel assured he has no power to come upon earth to deceive us and entice our souls from the good God who created this beautiful world, and who alone can govern men and events."

Landry, gradually surmounting his foolish fear, could not help observing how in all ways Fanchon was a good Christian; her devotion even appeared to him more beautiful than that of others, for she loved the Almighty with all the strength of her soul, and, as she spoke of this love to Landry, he was surprised and ashamed to find how little he understood the prayers and precepts he had been taught, and which a feeling of duty only had led him to respect, his heart remaining untouched by that love for his Creator which distinguished Fanchon.

While thus frequenting her society he learned the properties of various herbs and became skilled in recipes for the cure of human beings and animals; nor was it long before he made a trial of that skill upon one of Caillaud's cows, which, having overeaten itself with green food, was pronounced incurable by the veterinary surgeon. Landry secretly administered a drink which Fanchon had taught him to concoct, and when the farm servants came the next morning to look for the dead cow they were surprised to find the animal still alive, its eye clear, and the swelling rapidly subsiding. On another occasion, a colt being bitten by a viper, Landry, still following the instructions of Fanchon, succeeded in saving it, and was even enabled to cure a mad dog of La Priche. As Landry still did his best to conceal his intimacy with Fanchon, he made no boast of his skill, and the cure of the animals was attributed solely to the care he had bestowed upon them. But Caillaud, who understood these matters well, as all good farmers should, was amazed, and thought to himself:

"Farmer Barbeau has no talent in this way, nor does he even possess good luck, for last year he lost a good many beasts, and not for the first time, either. Landry has a lucky hand, and this is a gift of nature; all the schooling in the world will never make up for its absence. He knows at a glance what to do, and such skill is better than capital in the management of a farm."

Caillaud's thoughts were not the thoughts of a

credulous or an ignorant man, only he was deceived in attributing to a gift of nature in Landry
what was the result of skill and judgment. Nevertheless these gifts of nature are no fables, for
Fanchon was thus endowed, and with a few lessons from her grandmother had been enabled to
divine properties in plants never before dreamed
of, and to apply these properties to their right
use. She was none the more a sorceress for this
and was right to defend herself from the charge,
though she had an observing and reflecting mind
—and that this is a gift of nature no one can deny.
Caillaud, however, pushed the matter a little
further. He believed that certain cowherds and
laborers, by virtue only of their presence in the
stable or field, brought good or evil to the animals or crops. And as there is always some truth
in the falsest belief, it must be granted that care,
cleanliness and conscientious labor possess a virtue for good, whilst negligence and stupidity destroy.

As Landry's thoughts and tastes had ever been
centered in such matters, the affection he had
conceived for Fanchon was increased by the
gratitude her owed her for her instruction, and
the esteem he acquired through her skill. It was
then for the first time he felt how right she had
been to divert his thoughts from love during their
long rambles and interviews, while he also recognized how she had taken the interests of her lover
more to heart than the pleasure of allowing her-

self to be caressed and courted, as he had at one time desired.

Landry at last was so deeply and earnestly in love that he trampled beneath his feet all shame for his devotion to a girl reputed ugly and badly disposed; and, if he still remained cautious, it was for the sake of Sylvinet, with whose jealous disposition he was only too well acquainted, and who had already made a great effort to become reconciled to his affection for Madelon, so tranquil and unimportant to that he now entertained for Fanchon Fadet. But if Landry were too much in earnest to be prudent, Fanchon, naturally disposed toward mystery, and anxious to avoid exposing Landry to the jests of his companions, in short, loving him too well to cause him trouble in his family, exacted from him so great a secrecy that more than a year passed away before the affair was discovered. Landry by degrees had accustomed Sylvinet no longer to watch his every movement; and a thinly peopled district, intersected by ravines and well covered with trees, is of all others favorable to lovers. Sylvinet, finding that Landry thought no more of Madelon— an affection which he had brought himself to look upon as a necessary evil, rendered lighter by the timidity of Landry and the reserve of the girl— greatly rejoiced that he was not called upon to share his brother's heart with a rival, and being freed from jealousy, left Landry more free to his occupations and pleasures. Pretexts were not wanting to Landry for coming and going, and every Sunday evening he would quit his father's house at an early hour—not to return to La Priche, but to linger with Fanchon till midnight, having succeeded in getting his bed removed to an out-door room, where he could enter at any hour he pleased without disturbing the family. From the Sunday to the Monday morning his time was his own, Caillaud and his son taking upon themselves the whole care of the farm, that, as they said, the young people who worked harder than they during the week, might on the Sabbath enjoy themselves freely, according to the ordinance of God.

During winter, when the nights are so cold that courting in the open fields becomes a matter of difficulty, there was good shelter for Landry and Fanchon in an old dove-cote, long abandoned by the birds, but well covered in, which belonged to Caillaud's farm. At times it served to hold the surplus of his crops; and, as Landry had the key, and it was situated on the confines of the grounds of La Priche, not far from the ford of Roulettes, in the middle of an enclosed field, any one must have been cunning indeed to surprise the meeting of the two young lovers. When the weather would allow they preferred wandering among the copse-wood, with which that part of the country is covered, and which upon occasion can furnish an excellent retreat for thieves or lovers; but, as there were no thieves thereabouts, the lovers only availed themselves of it to their hearts' content.

CHAPTER XVIII.

But as no secret can be kept forever, one fine Sunday morning our lovers were detected. Sylvinet, passing along the churchyard wall, heard the voice of his twin a few steps from him, and though Landry spoke softly, Sylvinet knew his every tone so well that he could have guessed the words had he not heard them spoken.

"Why will you not dance?" he said to some one whom Sylvinet was unable to see. "It is so long since you have remained after mass that no one will take any notice of my dancing with you now; or, if they do, instead of attributing it to love, they will suppose I am curious to know if, after so long an interval, you can still dance well."

"No, Landry, no," replied a voice which Sylvinet failed to recognize, in the length of time which had elapsed since he last heard it, Fanchon having kept herself aloof from him in particular. "No," said she, "you must not draw attention upon me; it is better as it is, for if I dance with you once you will wish me to do so every Sunday, and people are easily set talking. Believe what I have already said, Landry, that on the day it is known you love me our troubles will commence. Let me go now, and when you have spent a portion of the day with your family and your brother you can come and meet me where we have agreed."

"It is very provoking that we can never dance!" said Landry. "You love dancing dearly and you dance so well. What delight it would give me to watch you moving so lightly and gracefully, and to know that you would dance with no one but me."

"And this is just what we must avoid," said she. "But I see you regret not dancing, my good Landry, and I know no reason why you should renounce it. Join the dancers for a while; it will give me pleasure to think you are amusing yourself, and I shall wait for you patiently."

"Oh! your patience is too great!" said Landry, in a voice which showed the absence of it in himself. "I would rather cut off my legs than dance with a girl I do not love, and whom I would not kiss for a hundred francs!"

"Well, if I dance at all," said Fanchon, "I must dance with others beside you, and must allow myself to be kissed like the rest."

"Then you shall not dance at all," said Landry, quickly. "I will not have any one else kiss you."

Sylvinet heard nothing more but the sound of retreating footsteps, and that he might not be found listening by his brother, who was coming in his direction, he entered the churchyard till he had passed.

This discovery was a terrible blow to poor Sylvinet. He did not care to know the girl whom Landry loved so passionately. It was enough to know that some one existed for whom Landry forsook him, and who held such entire possession of his thoughts that all confidence in his brother was destroyed.

"He must distrust me," thought he; "and this girl whom he loves so dearly teaches him to fear and detest me.   I am no longer suprised at his weariness at home, or his uneasiness when I wish to walk with him.   I gave up this pleasure, believing he wished to be alone, and I shall take good care for the future not to annoy him.   I shall keep my discovery to myself, for he would only be vexed at my knowing what he does not wish to confide to me.   I shall suffer in silence, while he rejoices at being rid of me."

Sylvinet carried this resolution into effect, and even went further than was at all necessary, for he not only sought no longer to retain his brother with him, but, that he might not be in his way, he was himself the first to quit the house, seeking some solitary spot where there was no danger of an encounter.

"Were I to meet Landry," thought he, "he would imagine I watched his movements, and would take care to let me know I was in the way."

Thus by degrees the old grief, of which he had been almost cured, returned with such obstinacy and strength that it was not long before evidences of it were to be seen in his face.   His mother quietly reproached him, but at eighteen he was ashamed of the weakness he had not sought to conceal three years earlier, and he refused to confess the cause of his annoyance.

It was this, however, which saved him from ill-

ness; for God abandons only those who abandon
themselves; and he who has courage to conceal
his grief is stronger to combat it than he who
complains.   The unfortunate boy grew pale and
sad; from time to time an attack of fever seized
him, so that, though still growing slowly, he remained slight and delicate in appearance.   He
was not strong enough to endure much work, yet
thinking it sufficient to grieve his father by his
sadness, and being unwilling to add to that grief
by any appearance of laziness he frequently
worked beyond his strength, undertaking more
than he could bear, and on the morrow finding
himself unable to move.

"Sylvinet will never make a good laborer," said
Barbeau, "but he does his best, and does not always spare himself enough, and this is why I do
not like to send him away from home; for, between his dread of reproach, and the little
strength God has given him, he would soon kill
himself outright, and I should never forgive myself as long as I lived."

Mother Barbeau agreed perfectly in this
opinion, and did her best to soothe and enliven
Sylvinet.   She consulted several physicians concerning his health, some of whom told her she
must take great care of her boy, and give him
nothing but milk to drink, as he was exceedingly
weak and delicate; while others said that he must
be made to work, and drink good wine, because
being feeble, he needed everything to strengthen
him.   Now, between the two, as is often the case

when more than one person at a time is consulted,
Mother Barbeau knew not what to do. Fortunately she followed the advice of neither, and
Sylvinet went on in his own way, bearing his trials
with more fortitude than of old, till Landry's love
for Fanchon becoming generally known, he found
his own sorrows doubled by the sorrows of his
brother.

It was Madelon who effected the discovery, and
if this were the result of accident, no one can
deny that she made a bad use of it afterwards.
Never having loved Landry, she was quickly consoled for his loss, though there remained in her
heart a rancorous feeling, which wanted only an
opportunity to make itself felt; so true is it that
the anger of a woman outlives her regret.

It was thus the matter came to pass. The beautiful Madelon, renowned for her prudent bearing
and haughty manners with the young men of the
village, was nevertheless a coquette at heart, and
not half so discriminating and faithful in her affections as the poor Cricket, of whom every one
spoke ill, and foretold worse. Madelon had already had two lovers, without reckoning Landry,
when she favored a third in the person of her
cousin, the eldest son of Farmer Caillaud. To
wards him she showed such evident favor, that
finding herself watched by her last lover, to whom
she had also given encouragement, and fearing
he would raise a scandal at her expense, she allowed herself to be persuaded by her cousin to
meet him in the very dove-cote, whither Landry

and Fanchon were accustomed to repair. Cadet
Caillaud, after seeking everywhere in vain for
the key of this place, which Landry carried in his
pocket, resolved to break in the door; and it so
happened, that at the time he carried this resolution into effect, Landry and Fanchon were there.
The four lovers, as may well be imagined, looked
foolish enough at this unexpected encounter; but
the mutual discovery should have bound them to
mutual silence.

Madelon, however, experienced a return of
jealousy and anger at the sight of Landry, who
had become one of the handsomest young men in
the country, and finding that since the fete of
Saint Andoche he had remained true to Fanchon,
she determined to be avenged. To this end, without confiding her determination to Cadet Caillaud, who was an honest, good-hearted fellow, and
would not have lent himself to it, she procured the
assistance of two or three young girls, who, also
piqued at the contempt in which Landry seemed
to hold them by never inviting them to dance, set
about watching the little Fanchon to such purpose that it was not long before they became con-
vinced of her attachment to Landry. Having
once or twice seen the lovers together, they
spread the news through the country, telling all
who would listen to them—and slander never
wants tongue to repeat it, or ears to listen—that
Landry was carrying on an intrigue with Fanchon.

Upon this all the young women in the neighborhood joined in the outcry; for when a rich and handsome youth devotes himself exclusively to one woman, the rest look upon it as an insult to themselves, and if blame can be imputed to that woman, let her look to it in time! Be sure that a wrong-doing, discovered by a woman, will travel far and near. Thus, one fortnight after the adventure at the dove-cote, Madelon, taking good care that her name should never be mentioned in connection with it, every one, both great and small, old and young, knew of the love of Landry, the twin, for Fanchon Fadet, the Cricket.

The scandal at length reached the ears of Mother Barbeau, who, though greatly afflicted in consequence, dared not mention the subject to her good man. However, Barbeau learned it elsewhere, and Sylvinet, who had faithfully preserved his brother's secret, had the grief of finding that every one knew it.

One evening as Landry, according to custom, was about to leave home at an early hour, his father said to him, in the presence of his mother, eldest sister, and his twin brother:

"Do not be in a hurry to leave us, Landry, for I have something to say to you, but I must wait till your godfather arrives, for it is in the presence of those members of the family who take most interest in your fate, I desire to ask an explanation."

And when the godfather, that is, Uncle Landriche, had arrived, Barbeau continued in the following manner:

"What I have to say will, I fear, cause you some shame, Landry, for it is not without shame and regret I find myself called upon to expose you before your family. But I believe that this shame will be of service to you, and help to cure you of a fancy which may lead to much harm. It appears you have formed an unlucky acquaintance, dating from the last fete of St. Andoche, now nearly a twelvemonth ago. I have heard a good deal of it from the first, for it was a curious thing to find you dancing a whole day with the dirtiest, ugliest, and least reputable girl of these parts, but I did not pay much attention to it, thinking you were only in fun; though I did not exactly approve of your conduct, since, if we must not frequent the company of bad people, neither must we expose them to humiliation and disgrace. I neglected to speak of it to you, thinking, when I saw you out of spirits on the morrow, that your conscience reproached you, and that you would behave so no more. But, during the past week, I have heard quite a different tale, and that from persons worthy of credit, though I will not believe what is told me till you confirm it. If I suspect you wrongly, you must impute my error to the interest I feel in you, and to the duty which is binding upon me to watch your conduct. If the tale be false, it will give me great pleasure to hear you say so, and to know that you have been wronged in my opinion."

"My father," said Landry, "will you tell me of

what I am accused, and I will reply according to the truth, and the respect I owe you."

"You are accused, Landry, as I thought I had given you to understand, of an intrigue with the granddaughter of Mother Fadet, who is herself a woman of sufficiently bad character, without taking into consideration that the mother of this unfortunate girl wickedly forsook her husband, her children, and her home, to follow the soldiers. You are accused of wandering hither and thither with Fanchon, which makes me fear you are engaged in some disgraceful affair, of which you may have cause to repent through the whole course of your life. Do you understand now?"

"I understand your perfectly, my dear father," replied Landry; "but allow me one question before I reply. Is it because of her family, or on account of herself, that you look upon Fanchon Fadet as a bad acquaintance for me?"

"Both reasons weigh with me, beyond doubt," returned Barbeau, with more severity in his tone than he had at first used, for he had expected to find Landry confused, whereas he was calm and collected, and, as it seemed, prepared for the worst. "First of all," said he, "her parentage is a villainous blot, and never could a family, esteemed and respected like our own, endure to form an alliance with the family of Fadet. Secondly, Fanchon, in herself, inspires neither respect nor esteem. She has been brought up under our eyes, and w know exactly what she is. It is true I have heard that, during the past year, she has

10

greatly improved, and no longer runs wild about
the country. You see I have no wish to deny
her justice; but this improvement is not enough
to make me believe that a girl so badly brought
up can ever make an honest woman. Knowing
the grandmother as I do, I have every reason to
fear that there is some plan afloat to extract promises from you, which, fulfilled, will overwhelm
you with shame and disgrace. I am even now
told that matters have gone so far as to render
an action probable, if you now withdraw."

Landry, who, from the first, had determined to
be forbearing and prudent, now lost all patience.
His face as red as fire, he rose, saying:

"Father, whoever has told you this has told a
lie, and has so wronged and insulted Fanchon
Fadet, that, were he here, he should eat his words,
or fight me to the death! Tell him, from me, that
he is a coward, and that, if ever we meet he shall
answer for his falsehood and villainy!"

"Pray do not be so violent, Landry," said Sylvinet, overcome with grief; "my father does not
accuse you of having wronged the girl, but he
fears lest, in her intimacy with you, she may become compromised, and you may feel bound to
offer her the only reparation in your power."

CHAPTER XIX.

THE voice of his twin somewhat soothed Landry, though he could not allow the words he uttered to pass unchallenged.

"Brother," said he, "you do not understand these matters. You were always prejudiced against Fanchon, and you know nothing about her. I care not for what is said of me, but I will not allow her to be ill spoken of, and I desire that my father and mother should learn from me that there is not in the whole world another girl so good, honest, and unselfish as Fanchon Fadet. If she have the misfortune to come of bad parentage, all the more credit is due to her for being what she is, and I never would have believed that any one could be found so unchristian as to reproach her for her birth."

"Do you mean to reproach me, Landry?" said Barbeau, also rising, that he might put an end to the conversation between them. "I see, by your anger, that you are more interested in this Fanchon than I could desire; and, as you feel neither shame nor regret in the matter, we will talk of it no more. I shall consider how best to save you from the consequences of a youthful indiscretion. It is time now to return to your master."

"You must not leave us thus," said Sylvinet, detaining his brother, as he was about to go. "Lan-

dry is so grieved, father, at having vexed you,
that he has not a word to utter. Forgive him, or
he will weep the whole night, and will suffer
cruelly from your displeasure."

Sylvinet wept as he spoke; Mother Barbeau
wept also; and the eldest sister and Uncle Landriche kept them company. Only Barbeau and
Landry had dry eyes, but their hearts were full,
and they embraced each other in silence. The
father, being unwilling to compromise his authority, exacted no promise, knowing that in all love
affairs promises are vain; but he gave Landry to
understand that the matter was not at an end, and
Landry departed, irritated and in despair. Sylvinet would gladly have followed him, had he
dared, but, presuming that his brother would at
once seek Fanchon, he went to bed, sad and unhappy, to dream of this family misfortune.

Landry repaired to the house of Fanchon
Fadet. and knocked gently at her door. Mother
Fadet had become so deaf, that once asleep, nothing could wake her; and, ever since the discovery
in the dove-cote, Landry had only been able to
converse with Fanchon of an evening, in the
room where slept the old woman and little Jeanot.
Even there he ran a great risk, for the old sorceress could not endure him, and, had she chanced
to see him, would have driven him out with blows.
Landry related his trouble to Fanchon, and, to his
surprise, found her resigned and courageous. At
first she tried to persuade him to forget his love
and to think no more about her; but when she

saw that this advice only added to his affliction and distress, she urged him to submit, and to put his trust in the future.

"Listen, Landry," she said to him; "I have always foreseen what has come to pass, and I have often thought what we should do when the time arrived. Your father is not in the wrong, and nothing will ever make me think so, for it is his affection for you which makes him fear to find you entangled with a person so undeserving as myself. I forgive him his pride and injustice towards me, for we cannot deny that my conduct has been foolish. You reproached me with it yourself the first day you loved me. We must allow some time yet to pass, and by degrees the prejudice against me will die away, the wicked falsehoods recently invented will fall of themselves. Your father and mother will soon see that I am discreet, and that I have no desire to seduce you into harm. They will in time render justice to the honesty of my affection, and we shall then be able to meet and converse with each other, without any further concealment. Meanwhile you must obey your father, who will, I feel sure, forbid you to see me."

"I shall never have the courage to do so," said Landry; "I would rather throw myself into the river."

"If that be the case, I must find courage for you," returned Fanchon; "I will take the matter into my own hands. I will quit these parts for a time. During the last three months a good

situation has been offered me in the town. My
grandmother is so old and deaf that she rarely
prescribes or administers medicine, and a relative
has long offered to live with her, and to take
charge both of her and of my poor little Grasshopper"——

At the thought of leaving this child, Fanchon's
voice trembled, for, save Landry, he was the only
one in the world whom she loved; but she took
courage and proceeded:

"He is strong enough now to do without me.
He is about to take his first communion, and the
necessity of attending his examination with other
children will serve to divert his grief at my departure. You must have observed how reasonable he has become of late, and how seldom his
companions now tease and enrage him. In
short, Landry, the people here must have time to
forget me. There is at present a strong prejudice
against me, but after one or two years of absence,
when I shall return with a good character and
an honest name, both of which I can acquire
easier elsewhere than here, we shall no longer
find opposition and annoyance, and shall love
each other better than ever for the sacrifice we
shall have made."

Landry would not listen to this proposal; he
was in despair, and returned to La Priche in a
state of mind which would have excited pity in
the hardest heart.

Two days after, as they were employed at the
vintage, Cadet Caillaud said to him:

"I see, Landry, you are displeased with me, and that for some time past you have scarcely spoken to me. Doubtless you think it was I who spread the report of your love for Fanchon, but I am sorry you should believe me capable of so base an act. As true as heaven above us, I have never breathed a word concerning it, and I regret deeply that all this annoyance should be brought upon you. I have ever esteemed you greatly, and never, by word or deed, have I injured Fanchon. Indeed, I may say, with truth, that I have esteemed her also ever since the adventure in the dove-cote, about which she has remained silent, when it was in her power to be avenged on Madelon, whom she well knows to be the author of all this scandal. I see clearly, Landry, that we must not trust to appearance and reputation. Fanchon, who is held to be wicked, has proved herself good; while Madelon, who is believed to be good, has behaved treacherously, not only towards you and Fanchon, but in giving me cause to doubt her fidelity."

Landry frankly accepted this explanation of Cadet Caillaud, who did all in his power to cheer and console him.

"A great deal of trouble has been brought upon you, my dear Landry," said he, in conclusion; "but you must find consolation in the admirable conduct of your Fanchon. It is a brave thing in her to go away for a time, that she may put an end to the trouble in your family, and I told her as much just now as I bid her good-bye."

"What do you say, Cadet?" exclaimed Landry; "Fanchon gone—departed?"

"Did you not know it?" returned Cadet. "I thought it had been agreed upon between you, and that it was to escape further blame you did not escort her. But she is gone to a certainty, for she passed to the right of our house, not a quarter of an hour ago, with her bundle under her arm. She is going to Chateau-Meillant, but she cannot have got very far on her road."

Landry left his work, and never paused till he had overtaken Fanchon; then, exhausted by his haste and the violence of his grief, he fell across the road, unable to speak, but making signs to let her know that she must walk over his body if she still persisted in leaving him.

When he had somewhat recovered, Fanchon said to him:

"I wished to spare you this sorrow, my dear Landry, and here you are doing all you can to deprive me of courage. Be a man, and do not take all heart from me; I require all the strength you can give me. And when I reflect that my poor little Jeanot is at this very moment seeking after me, with tears and lamentations, I feel so weak, so miserable, that for a little more I could hurl myself against these stones. Oh, I beseech you, Landry, assist me to do my duty, instead of trying to turn me from it; for if I do not go now I shall never go at all, and we are lost."

"Fanchon, Fanchon, you do not need more courage," said Landry. "Your regrets are only

for a child, who, because he is a child, will quickly
be consoled. You do not heed my despair; you
do not know what love is; you do not love me,
and will soon forget me, if, indeed, you ever return."

"I shall return, Landry; I take heaven to witness that I shall return in one year at the soon-
est, in two years at the latest, and so far from forgetting you, I will have neither friend nor lover
save yourself."

"No other friend, perhaps, Fanchon, because
you will never find another so submissive as myself; but for another lover, I know not who can
answer for that?"

"I can," said Fanchon, calmly, but firmly.

"You cannot, Fanchon, for you have never
loved; and when you do, you will soon forget your
poor Landry. Oh, if you loved me as I love
you, you would never forsake me thus."

"Do you think so?" said Fanchon, looking at
him with a sad and serious expression. "Perhaps you know not what you are saying. For
my own part, I think love, even more than friendship, commands me to depart."

"Ah, Fanchon, if it be love which commands
you to depart, I should not be so grieved; I should
be almost happy in my misfortunes; I should
have faith in your word, and would hope for the
future; I should feel the courage which animates
you. But it is not love; you have told me so
often, and your tranquility by my side has con-
firmed your words."

"So you believe it is not love," said Fanchon. "You feel assured of it?"

And still looking at him, her eyes filled with large tears, which rolled down her cheeks, as she smiled with a peculiar expression.

"Oh, Heaven! if I am only mistaken!" cried Landry, throwing his arms around her.

"I believe you are indeed mistaken," replied Fanchon, still smiling and weeping. "From thirteen years of age the poor Cricket has thought of Landry, and of no one but him; and when she followed him through the roads and fields, teasing him with follies and nonsense, though, unknown to herself, I believe, it was only to attract his attention. I believe, that on the day she set about seeking for Sylvinet, and found him, sad and pensive, at the brink of the river, with a lamb in his arms, she played the sorceress with Landry, only to secure his gratitude. I believe that when she insulted him at the ford of Roulette, it was in anger and vexation at his subsequent neglect, and that in her infatuation she desired to dance with him, hoping to secure his admiration of her skill and agility. I believe that when Landry found her weeping in the road, it was from repentance and sorrow at having incurred his displeasure. I believe, also, that when he desired to kiss her, and she refused, when he spoke of love, and she replied in words of friendship, it was from fear that she might lose that love by returning it too quickly. In short, I believe that her present departure, lacerating as it is to her own heart, is in the hope that she may return worthy of Landry in the eyes of the world, to become his wife, without bringing sorrow and disgrace upon his family."

At these words Landry felt as though he must go mad with joy. He laughed, he cried, he wept, he kissed Fanchon's hand, her dress, and would even have kissed her feet, but raising him gently in her arms, she imprinted on his lips the first kiss she had ever given him, and, as he fell fainting to the ground, overcome with surprise and emotion, she picked up her bundle, and, blushing and confused, made her escape, forbidding him to follow, but promising faithfully to return.

CHAPTER XX.

LANDRY submitted, and returned to the vineyard, greatly surprised at not finding himself so unhappy as he had expected, so sweet is it to know oneself beloved, and so great is the faith of a true and devoted affection. So surprised and happy was he, that he could not help speaking of it to Cadet Caillaud, who shared in his surprise, and admired Fanchon for having had the strength to overcome all weakness and imprudence during the time she had loved Landry, and had known herself loved in return.

"I am glad to see," said he, "that this girl has so many good qualities; for, as far as I am con-

cerned, I never judged ill of her; and I must own
that, if she had thought me worthy of attention,
I should not have been displeased. Her eyes
have always made her seem to me more beautiful than ugly, and, for some time past, it has been
very evident that she was becoming every day
more agreeable and pleasing. But she loved you
exclusively, Landry, and was satisfied if she did
not displease others; she sought no approbation
but yours, and I can assure you a woman of this
kind would have suited me admirably. Besides,
young and foolish as I have known her, I always
considered she had a good heart; and if any one
were asked to say conscientiously and in truth
what he thought and knew of her disposition, he
would be obliged to bear witness in her favor;
but the world is so framed, that when two or
three persons join against another to form a bad
reputation, the crowd, without knowing why, follow the lead, as though for the simple pleasure of
crushing what is defenceless."

Landry found great comfort in hearing Cadet
Caillaud reason thus, and from that day he
formed a great friendship for him, and consoled
himself in a measure for his griefs, by confiding
them to him; he even said to him, one day:

"Think no more of this Madelon, who is worth-
less, and who has caused us both sorrow, my
brave Cadet. You are of my own age, and there
is no hurry about your marrying. Now I have a
little sister, Nanette, who is pretty, well brought
up, gentle, loving, and nearly sixteen years old.

Come and see us oftener; my father greatly esteems you, and when you come to know our Nanette, you will see that you cannot entertain a better thought than that of becoming my brother-in-law."

"I will not say no to such a proposition," returned Cadet, "and if she is not already engaged I will go home with you every Sunday."

On the evening of the departure of Fanchon Fadet, Landry wished to go and see his father, to let him know the honest conduct of this girl, of whom he had judged so ill, and at the same time to offer him, with no provisions for the future, his submission for the present. His heart swelled within him as he passed the house of Mother Fadet; but he armed himself with courage by thinking that, were it not for the departure of Fanchon he might perhaps have remained for some time longer in ignorance that he was beloved by her. He saw the Mother Fanchette, who was the relation and godmother of Fanchon, and who had come to look after the old woman and the child in her place. She was sitting before the door, with the Grasshopper upon her knees. The poor Jeanot was crying and refusing to go to bed, because his Fanchon had not yet returned, and it was she who must hear his prayers and put him to sleep. Mother Fanchette did her best to comfort him, and Landry with pleasure heard her speaking in a gentle and affectionate tone. But as soon as the Grasshopper saw Landry passing he escaped from the hands

of Fanchette, at the risk of leaving one of his
feet behind him, and ran to throw himself into the
arms of the twin, kissing, questioning, and con-
juring him to bring back his Fanchon.   Landry
embraced him, and, himself shedding tears, consoled him as best he could.   He offered him a
bunch of grapes from the basket which he was
carrying, as a present from Mother Caillaud to
his own family; but Jeanot, though somewhat of
a gourmand, would not have any, unless Landry
promised to go and fetch his Fanchon, to which
request Landry was obliged to feign submission,
that he might induce the child to submit to
Mother Fanchette.

Barbeau did not anticipate such a step on the
part of Fanchon.   He was satisfied with it,
though, so good and just a man was he at heart;
he could not help feeling something like regret
at what he had done.

"I am sorry, Landry," said he, "that you had
not the courage to give up associating with her.
Had you acted according to your duty, you would
not have been the cause of her departure.   God
grant that this child may not have to suffer in her
new position, and that her absence may not be injurious to her grandmother and her little brother;
for, if many speak ill of her, there are also some
who defend her, and who assure me that she is
good and dutiful towards her family.   If what I
have heard injurious to her be a falsehood, we
shall soon know it, and we will defend her as we
ought; if, unfortunately, it prove true, and you

are culpable, Landry, we will assist her, and will not allow her to fall into misery and want. That you will never marry her, Landry, is all I exact."

"My father," said Landry, "you and I judge things differently. Were I guilty of what you think, I should, on the contrary, ask your permission to marry her. But, as Fanchon is as innocent as my sister, Nanette, I ask nothing of you now but forgiveness for the sorrow I have caused you. We will speak of Fanchon at some future time, as you have promised."

Barbeau was obliged to accept this condition, and to press the matter no further. He was too prudent to drive things to extremity, and was obliged to be content with what he had obtained.

From that time there was no further question of Fanchon at the Bessonniere. They even avoided mentioning her altogether, for Landry turned red and white when her name chanced to escape any one's lips before him, and it was easy to see that he cherished her remembrance as much as ever.

At first Sylvinet experienced a species of egotistical gratification in learning of the departure of Fanchon, as he flattered himself that henceforth his twin would love only him, and would never quit him for another. But it was not so. Sylvinet was indeed the one whom Landry loved best after Fanchon, but he could not find pleasure for long in his society, since Sylvinet would not abate his aversion for Fanchon. Whenever Landry tried to speak of her to him, to enlist him in their interest, Sylvinet fretted, and reproached him for persevering in an idea so repugnant to their parents and so grievous to him. Thenceforth Landry mentioned the subject to him no more; but, as he could not live without speaking of Fanchon, he divided his time between Cadet Caillaud and the little Jeanot, whom he took out to walk with him, making him repeat his catechism, and instructing and consoling him as well as he could. Had they dared, when he was seen with this child, the lads would have mocked him; but, besides that Landry never allowed any one to make game of him, he was rather proud than ashamed of showing his affection for the brother of Fanchon Fadet, thus protesting against those who said that Farmer Barbeau, in his sagacity, had soon put an end to the love affair between Fanchon and his son. Sylvinet, seeing that his brother did not seek him as often as he could have wished, and finding himself obliged to transfer his jealousy to the little Jeanot and Cadet Caillaud; seeing, moreover, that his sister, Nanette, who, until then, had always consoled and cheered him by gentle and affectionate attentions, was beginning to take great pleasure in the society of her brother's friend, an inclination which both families strongly approved; poor Sylvinet, whose fancy it was to possess exclusively the affection of those whom he loved, fell into a state of mortal despair, while his mind became so gloomy that no one ever knew how to appease him. He scarcely ever laughed, took no pleasure in anything about him, and could hardly work, so consumed and weakened was he by this devouring jealousy. At last fears for his life were entertained, for the fever seldom left him; and, when suffering more than usual, he would say things cruelly afflicting to the hearts of his parents. He pretended that no one loved him—he, who had always been more petted and spoiled than the rest of the family. He wished for death, saying that he was good for nothing; that they humored him from compassion for his state, but that he was a burden to his family, and that the greatest mercy the good God could show would be to relieve them of him.

Sometimes Barbeau, overhearing these unchristian words, would reprove him severely; but this did no good. At others, he conjured him, with tears, better to appreciate his affection. This was still worse; Sylvinet wept, repented, asked pardon of his father, mother, his twin, and all his family; and then, having given way to the overtenderness of his sick heart, the fever would return worse than ever. The doctors were consulted afresh, but could give no advice. It was easy to see that they attributed the mischief to the twinship, which must inevitably kill one or the other. They also consulted the bathwoman of Clavieres, the wisest woman in the canton, next to La Sagette, who was dead, and the Mother Fadet, who was in her second childhood. This skillful person replied to Mother Barbeau:

11

"Only one thing can save your child, and that is love for a woman."

"And that is just what he cannot endure the thought of," said Mother Barbeau. "Never was there a boy so proud and cold; and, since the moment his twin took love into his head, he has done nothing but speak ill of all the girls of our acquaintance. He blames all, because one among them (and unfortunately not the best) has taken from him, as he pretends, his brother's heart."

"Well," said the old woman, whose knowledge of the maladies both of body and mind was very great, "your son Sylvinet, when he does love a woman, will love her more extravagantly than he loves his brother. I foretell this. There is a superabundance of affection in his heart, and having always bestowed it upon his twin, he has almost forgotten his sex; and by so doing he has violated the law of the good God, who ordains that a man shall cherish a wife more than father or mother, brothers or sisters. Console yourself, however. It is impossible but that nature will sooner or later speak within him, and when once he loves, whether the girl be rich or poor, good or bad, do not hesitate to give her to him in marriage, for according to all appearances, he will love only once during his whole life. His heart has too much constancy for a second attachment, and as it will need a miracle of nature to separate him from his twin, it will need a greater still to separate him from the person who shall supplant him."

This advice appeared very sensible to Barbeau, and he tried to induce Sylvinet to visit at the houses where there were good and handsome girls, of a marriageable age. But, though Sylvinet was a good-looking and well-conducted youth, his sad, cold air was not calculated to touch the hearts of the girls. They made no advances, and he, in his timidity, imagined that in fearing he detested them.

Upon this, Caillaud, who was the great friend and one of the best advisers of the family, gave the following counsel:

"I have always told you," said he, "that absence was the best remedy. Look at Landry! He was madly in love with Fanchon, and yet she departed, and he has lost neither his reason nor his health; he is even less sad than he was before; we have all observed this, though we know not the cause, for he appears quite reasonable and submissive. It would be the same with Sylvinet if, for five or six months, he were to see nothing of his brother. I will tell you how to separate them easily. My farm of La Priche is going on well; but on the other hand, my paternal estate at Arthon is doing badly, since for the last year, my bailiff has been ill, and has not been able to attend to it. I do not wish to turn him away, for he is an excellent man. But if I could send him a good laborer to assist him, he would soon recover, seeing that his illness arises from fatigue and overwork. If you consent, I will send Landry for the rest of the season. We will get him off without telling Sylvinet that it is for any length of time; on the contrary, we will tell him that it is for eight days, and the eight days past, we will speak of eight days more, and so on, till he gets accustomed to his absence. Follow my advice, instead of always humoring the fancy of a child whom you have petted and spoiled among you."

Barbeau was inclined to follow this advice, but Mother Barbeau was frightened; she feared it would be a death-blow to Sylvinet; they were therefore obliged to compromise the matter. She demanded that they should first try if keeping Landry a fortnight in the house, his brother seeing him at all hours, would not effectually cure him. If not, then Caillaud's advice was to be followed.

And so it was. Landry came to pass the required time at the Bessonniere, and they gave as a reason that his father wanted assistance to thrash the remainder of his corn, Sylvinet being no longer able to work. Landry took all possible pains to make his brother satisfied with him. He saw him at all hours, slept in the same bed, and watched over him as though he had been a child. The first day Sylvinet was joyous, but on the second day he pretended that Landry was tired of him, and Landry could not divest him of this idea. The third day Sylvinet was in a rage, because the Grasshopper came to see Landry, and Landry had not the heart to dismiss him. In short, at the end of a week they were obliged to give up the plan, for Sylvinet became more and more unjust, exacting, and jealous of his very shadow. Then, they thought of carrying into execution Caillaud's idea, and, though Landry, loving his home, his native place, his family, and his master, did not desire to go to Arthon among strangers, he submitted to all that was advised, for the welfare of his brother.

CHAPTER XXI.

THE first day Sylvinet almost died with grief; but on the second he was more tranquil, and on the third the fever quitted him altogether. He appeared to resign himself to his fate; and, at the end of the week it was ascertained that the absence of his brother was better for him than his presence. In the jealousy to which he was secretly a prey he found a motive for being almost reconciled to the departure of Landry.

"At least," said he to himself, "in the place to which he is going, and where he knows no one, he will not so quickly form new friendships. He will be sad: he will think of me, and when he returns he will love me better than ever."

It was three months from the time of Landry's departure, and about a year since Fanchon had quitted the country, when she suddenly returned, her grandmother having become paralyzed. She nursed her with great affection and zeal; but age is the most hopeless of maladies, and at the end of a fortnight Mother Fadet gave up the ghost. Three days after, having attended the corpse of the poor old woman to the churchyard, having arranged the house, undressed and put her little brother to bed, and kissed her good godmother, who had retired to rest in another apartment, Fanchon was sitting, sadly, before a small fire, which scarcely threw out any heat, listening to the song of the cricket in the chimney, and thinking of her lover, as the rain drove against the window, when some one knocked at the door, and a voice said:

"Fanchon Fadet, are you there, and do you know who I am?"

She was not slow in obeying the summons, and great was her joy in being pressed to the heart of her friend Landry. Landry had heard of the illness of the grandmother and the return of Fanchon, and being unable to resist the desire of seeing her, had come at night, to depart again at the break of day. They passed the time by the fireside, in calm and serious conversation, for Fanchon reminded Landry that the bed on which her grandmother had yielded up her soul was scarcely cold, and that it was neither the hour nor the place to give way to their happiness. But, spite of their good intentions, they were delighted to be together again, and to find that they loved each other better than ever. As daylight ap-

proached Landry began to lose courage, and implored Fanchon to conceal him somewhere, that
he might see her on the following night. But,
as usual, she led him back to reason. She gave
him to understand that they would no longer be
separated for any length of time, as she had made
up her mind to remain at home.

"I have reasons for this," said she, "which I
will let you know by and by, and which do not
affect my hopes of our marriage. Go and finish
the work your master has confided to you, since,
as my godmother tells me, it is necessary for the
cure of your brother that he should not see you
for some time to come."

"It is that thought only which induces me to
quit you," replied Landry; "for my poor twin has
already caused me much unhappiness, and I fear
will cause me still more. You, who are so wise,
Fanchon, ought surely to find some means of
curing him."

"I know no other means than moral ones," returned she, "for it is his mind which makes his
body sick; and whoever can cure the one will cure
the other. Bue he entertains such an aversion
for me that I shall never have an opportunity of
speaking to him, and giving him advice."

"And yet you are so clever, Fanchon, you
speak so well, you have so peculiar a gift for per-
suading one to do as you please, when you will
take the trouble, that were you to speak to him
only for an hour, you would do him good. Try
it, I implore you. Do not be repulsed by his

pride and ill-temper. Oblige him to listen to you.
Make this effort for my sake, Fanchon, and for
the success of our love also, for the opposition of
my brother will not be among the least of our dif-
ficulties."

Fanchon promised, and the lovers parted, after
having repeated over and over that they loved
each other and would continue to do so for ever
and ever.

No one knew of Landry's visit. Had Sylvinet
been aware of it he would have fallen ill again,
and would never have forgiven his brother for
coming to see Fanchon without seeing him.

Two days after, Fanchon, dressing herself neatly—for being no longer without means, her
mourning was of good material and make—set
out to walk through the streets of La Cosse; but,
as she had grown considerably, it was some time
before any one recognized her. Her sojourn in the
city had also improved her looks, for being better
fed and lodged, she had acquired a complexion and
a color suitable to her age, and could no longer
be taken for a boy in disguise, so beautiful had
her figure become. Love and happiness had lent
to her face and person that indescribable charm,
which may be seen, but cannot be described. In
short, if she were not the prettiest girl in the
world, as Landry thought, she was certainly the
most pleasing in expression, the freshest, and perhaps the most charming of the whole province.

Carrying a large basket on her arm, she entered the Bessonniere, and asked to speak to

Farmer Barbeau.   Sylvinet was the first to see
her, and turned from her in displeasure.   But she
inquired after his father so frankly, that he was
obliged to reply, and conduct her to the barn,
where Barbeau was engaged in thrashing.   Fanchon having begged Barbeau to take her to some
place where she might speak to him in private, he
closed the doors of the barn, and told her she
could say all she desired.

Fanchon did not allow herself to be dismayed
by the cold manner of Barbeau, but seating herself on a pile of straw, while he followed her example, she thus spoke: "Farmer Barbeau, though
my deceased grandmother had an ancient grudge
against you, and you have always disliked me, it
is none the less true that I know you for the most
just and upright man in these parts.   There can
be but one opinion on this subject, and my grandmother herself, while blaming you for your pride,
rendered you the same justice.   Moreover, I
have, as you know, long entertained an affection
for your son Landry.   He has often spoken of
you to me, and I know from him, better than from
others, your real character and worth.   This is
why I have come to ask of you a service, and to
take you into my confidence."

"Speak, Fanchon," replied Barbeau.   "I have
never refused assistance to any one; and if my
conscience does not forbid in this instance, you
also may rely upon my services."

"This is what I want to consult you about,"
said Fanchon, raising her basket and placing it

between Barbeau's legs. "My deceased grandmother earned during her lifetime, by her medi-
cal advice and remedies, more money than was
believed; for as she spent scarcely anything, and
invested nothing, it was impossible to know the
amount she had concealed in a hole in her cellar,
which she often pointed out to me, saying:
'When I am no more, it is there you will find all
I have to leave you; it is your property, as well
as that of your brother; and if I stint you at present, it is that you may have all the more at some
future day; but do not let the lawyers meddle
with it, for they will spend it in expenses. Keep
it when you come into possession of it, conceal it
all your life, that it may serve you in your old age,
and that you may never know want.' Having
buried my poor grandmother, I obeyed her commands; I took the key of the cellar and loosened
the bricks of the wall, in the spot she had shown
me. There I found what I have brought you in
this basket, Farmer Barbeau, and which I beg
you to invest it as you think fit, after having satisfied the requirements of the law, of which I know
nothing."

"I thank you for your confidence, Fanchon,"
said Barbeau, without opening the basket,
though he felt a little curiosity; "but I have no
right to receive your money nor to superintend
your affairs. I am not your guardian. Doubtless your grandmother has made a will?"

"She has made no will, and the guardian the
law gives me, is my mother. Now, you know I

have heard nothing of her for a long time past, and I know not, poor soul, whether she be dead or alive. After her I have no relation but my godmother, Fanchette, who is an honest and a worthy woman, but altogether incapable of managing my money, or even keeping it safe. She would be unable to refrain from speaking of it, and showing it to every one, and I should fear either that she would make a bad investment, or that by allowing it to be handled by the curious, it would gradually diminish without her observing it; in short, my poor, dear godmother, is the last person fitted to take charge of it."

"Is it then a considerable sum?" asked Barbeau, whose eyes, in spite of himself, were fixed upon the cover of the basket. And as he spoke, he took it by the handle to feel the weight. But he found it so heavy, that he was astonished, and said: "If it be old iron, it will not take much to load a horse."

Fanchon, who was of a mischievous turn, was amused with his desire to see the contents of the basket. She pretended to open it, but Barbeau would have thought it beneath his dignity to allow her to do so.

"It does not concern me," he said, "and as I cannot take it in charge, I have no right to know anything about it."

"You must at least render me one little service, Farmer Barbeau," said Fanchon. "I am not much more clever than my godmother in reckoning anything but pence; I know not the value of all money, ancient or modern, and I can trust to no one but you to tell me whether I be rich or poor, and to know exactly the amount of my possessions."

"Come, then," said Barbeau, at last giving way, "it certainly is no great service you ask, and I ought not to refuse."

Upon this Fanchon slowly raised the double lids of the basket and drew forth a couple of large bags, each containing about two thousand French crown pieces.

"Ah, this is a pretty sum," said Barbeau; "here is a little fortune which will insure you plenty of lovers!"

"That is not all," said Fanchon; "there is still at the bottom of the basket, something of which I do not know the value."

And she drew forth an eel-skin purse, which she emptied into the hat of the farmer. It contained a hundred gold louis d'ors of ancient coinage, which made Barbeau's eyes open wide; and when he had counted and replaced them in the purse, she drew forth a second of the same value, and then a third, and then a fourth, till finally, in gold and silver and small money, there was in the basket not much short of forty thousand francs!

This was about a third in value more than all Barbeau's possessions in land and buildings; and, as country people scarcely ever realize large sums, he had never before seen so much money at a time.

Honest and disinterested as a peasant may be,

he cannot view a large amount of money undisturbed. Thus, for a moment, the perspiration
stood on his brow. When he had finished counting:

"You want but eight and twenty crowns," said
he, "of forty thousand francs, and one may say in
round numbers, that your share of the inheritance
is two thousand pistoles clear, which makes you
the best match in the country, Fanchon; and
your brother, the Grasshopper, can now afford to
be sickly and lame all his life, for he may ride
about in his carriage. Rejoice, then, for you may
consider yourself rich, and you have nothing to do
but make it known, to procure a handsome husband."

"I am in no hurry," said Fanchon; "on the contrary, I beg you to keep my wealth a secret,
Farmer Barbeau. I have a fancy, ugly as I am,
not to be married for my money, but for my good
heart and good fame; and as I have borne a bad
repute in these parts, I desire to pass some time
in them, that people may perceive I do not now
deserve it."

"As for your ugliness, Fanchon," said Barbeau, raising his eyes, which had not yet left the
precious basket, "I can tell you honestly that you
have devilishly improved, and that you are so
altered by your stay in the city, that you may pass
already for a good looking girl. And as for your
bad fame, if, as I would willingly think, you no
longer deserve it, I approve your idea of concealing your riches for a while, for there are not want-

ing those who, dazzled by your wealth, would
marry you, without entertaining for you that esteem which a woman ought to desire from her
husband.   Now, as to the deposit you wish to
make in my hands, it is against the law, and might
expose me hereafter to suspicions and accusations, for there is no lack of evil tongues; and,
besides, supposing you have the right to dispose
of what is your own, you have not the right to
dispose of what belongs to your brother, who is
still a minor.   All that I can do, is to seek advice for you without mentioning your name.   I
can then let you know the best means of invest-
ing your inheritance and that of your brother in
safety, without its passing through the hands of
lawyers, who are not always to be trusted.   Take
this money away, then, and conceal it again until
I can bring you a reply.   Should the necessity
occur, I will be a witness to the guardians of your
co-heritor, as to the amount of the sum we have
just counted, and which I will here write in a corner of my barn, that I may not forget it."

What Fanchon desired was that Barbeau
should know what she was worth.   If, in his presence, she felt proud at being rich, it was because
he could no longer accuse her of wishing to marry
Landry for his wealth.

CHAPTER XXII.

BARBEAU, finding Fanchon so prudent and intelligent, was less anxious to effect an investment of her funds than to inquire concerning the reputation she bore at Chateau-Meillant, where she had passed the last twelvemonth. For though this handsome fortune might tempt him to overlook the bad parentage of Fanchon, it could produce no effect where the honor of the girl whom he wished for a daughter-in-law was concerned. He therefore went to Chateau-Meillant, and conscientiously prosecuted his inquiries. He was told that Fanchon had conducted herself so admirably that not the smallest blame could be attached to her. She had served a religious old noblewoman, who had taken pleasure in making her a companion rather than a servant, so sensible, well conducted, and well-mannered, had she found her. The old lady regretted her loss greatly, and said that she was a perfect Christian, courageous, economical, neat, and careful, and of so amiable a disposition that she should never find her equal. And as this lady was rich, and gave a great deal away in charities, Fanchon had marvellously seconded her by nursing the sick, preparing medicaments, and by carrying into effect several valuable secrets with which her mistress had become acquainted in her convent life, before the revolution.

Barbeau was perfectly satisfied, and returned to La Cosse, determined to do justice to little Fanchon. He assembled his family, and charged his elder children, his brothers, and all his relations, to proceed prudently in an inquiry concerning the conduct of Fanchon since she had come to years of discretion, so that if the evil reports which had attached to her were grounded upon childish follies only, they might be taken for what they were worth; whereas, if any one could prove that he had seen her commit a bad action, or had known her to be guilty of any indecency, he should still be obliged to continue the prohibition he had laid on Landry against frequenting her society. The inquiry was conducted with the discretion he desired, and without the fact of her wealth being brought to light, upon which subject he said not a word, even to his wife.

During this time Fanchon lived very retired in her humble house, in which she made no change save in keeping it so clean that people might have seen their faces in her poor furniture. She also caused her little Grasshopper to be neatly dressed; and, without display, she provided for him, as well as for herself and her godmother, good nourishment, which quickly showed its effect on the child; he mended as fast as possible, and his health was soon as strong as could be desired. Happiness also produced a beneficial effect upon his temperament, and, being no longer threatened and punished by his grandmother, meeting only with caresses, gentle words and kind treatment, he became a good boy, full of drollery and good nature, no longer unpleasing to any, notwithstanding his lameness and his ugly little nose.

On the other hand so great a change took place in the person and habits of Fanchon Fadet that all evil reports were forgotten; and more than one lad, seeing her so graceful and sprightly, wished for the expiration of her mourning, that he might pay her attention and invite her to dance.

Sylvinet Barbeau was the only one who refused to alter his opinion. He saw clearly that something in connection with her was going on in the family, for his father could not forbear speaking of her frequently; and when Barbeau heard a denial to some old story circulated to the prejudice of Fanchon, he rejoiced for the sake of Landry, saying: "That he could not endure his son should be accused of betraying an innocent girl."

And then the return of Landry was spoken of, and Barbeau appeared to desire that Caillaud's consent should be obtained. In short, Sylvinet saw that there would no longer be any opposition to the love of Landry and Fanchon, and his chagrin returned. Opinion, which changes with every wind, had for a short time past set in favor of Fanchon; she was not, however, known to be rich, but she had grown pleasing, and for that was all the more displeasing to Sylvinet, who saw in her the rival of his love for Landry.

From time to time Barbeau allowed some word

12

concerning marriage to escape before Sylvinet, such as saying that the twins would soon be at an age to think of it. Landry's marriage had always been a thought of despair to Sylvinet, and, as it were, the final blow to their separation. His fever returned, and his mother anew consulted the doctors.

One day she met the godmother Fanchette, who, listening to her lamentations, asked her why she went so far to seek advice and spent so much money, when she had close to her a doctress more skillful than any in the country, and who did not practice for gain, like her grandmother, but for the love of God and her neighbor. Whereupon she named Fanchon the little Fadette.

Mother Barbeau mentioned this to her husband, who offered no opposition. He told her that at Chateau-Meillant Fanchon was held in great reputation for her skill, and that from all parts they came to consult her as much as her mistress.

Mother Barbeau therefore begged Fanchon to come and see Sylvinet, who was now confined to his bed, and to give him the benefit of her advice.

Fanchon had sought more than once for an opportunity of speaking to Sylvinet, in pursuance of her promise to Landry, but never had it arrived. She did not wait to be invited a second time, but hastened to see the poor twin. She found him in a feverish slumber, and begged the family to leave her alone with him. As it is the custom of wise women to act in secret, no one opposed her wishes and she was left as she desired.

First, Fanchon placed her hand on that of the twin, which was hanging over the side of the bed, but so gently that he did not perceive it, though his sleep was usually so light that the buzzing of a fly would awake him. Sylvinet's hand was hot as fire, and became hotter still in that of Fanchon. He evinced agitation, but without trying to release his hand. Then Fanchon placed her other hand on his forehead as gently as before, and his agitation increased. But by degrees he grew calm, and she felt the head and hand of her patient getting momentarily cooler, while his sleep became as calm as that of a little child. She remained thus by his side till she saw him disposed to awaken, when she drew behind the curtain and quitted the chamber and the house, saying to Mother Barbeau:

"Go and see your boy, and give him something to eat, for he has no longer any fever; but above all do not speak to him of me if you wish me to cure him. I will return this evening at the hour you tell me his malady is aggravated, and I will try again to overcome the fever."

Mother Barbeau was greatly astonished to find Sylvinet free from fever, and quickly gave him something to eat, of which he partook with a slight appetite; as this fever had not before left him for six days, and during that time he had refused to take anything, the skill of Fanchon was greatly admired, who, without waking him, without making him take any medicine, and by the simple virtue of her conjurations, as they thought, had already put him on the road to health.

Evening, however, brought back the fever, and with considerable violence. Sylvinet slumbered drowsily, wandering in his dreams, and when he awoke evinced terror of those around him.

Fanchon returned, and, as before, remained alone with him for an hour, using no other magic than that of gently holding his head and hands, cooling his hot face with her fresh breath.

Again she succeeded in relieving him from delirium and fever; and when she retired, still recommending that they should not mention her attendance to Sylvinet, they found him sleeping peacefully, his face no longer flushed, and presenting no appearance of illness.

I know not where Fanchon had picked up this idea. It must have come to her by chance and experience in the care of her little brother Jeanot, whom she had more than ten times rescued from death, using no other remedy than the refreshment of her hands and breath, warming him by the same means when the fever was followed by chills. She imagined that the affection and the will of a person in good health, the touch of a pure and vigorous hand, could drive away sickness, when that person was gifted with a certain intelligence and an unlimited confidence in the goodness of God. Thus, whenever she laid her hands on the sick she uttered in her soul some fervent prayer to the good God. And what she had often done for her little brother, and what she now did for the brother of Landry, she would not willingly have tried upon any less dear, or in whom she did not take an equal interest; for she believed that the great virtue of this remedy lay in the strong affection felt for the invalid, without which God gives no power over the malady. When Fanchon thus charmed the fever of Sylvinet she said to God in her prayer what she had said when she had charmed the fever of her brother: "My good God, cause the health of my body to pass into the body of this sufferer, and as the gentle Jesus offered Thee His life in the purchase of the souls of all human beings, if it be Thy will to take my life to give to this invalid, take it; I will surrender it willingly in exchange for the cure I implore."

Fanchon had thought of trying the virtue of this prayer by the death-bed of her grandmother, but she had not dared, since it seemed to her that the life of body and soul was becoming extinguished in this old woman by age and in obedience to the law of nature, which is the true will of God. And Fanchon, into whose charms, as it has been seen, more of religion than of deviltry entered, was afraid of displeasing Him by asking a thing not granted, save by miracle, to other Christians.

But, whether the remedy were useless or sovereign of itself, it is very certain that in three days she cured Sylvinet of his fever, and that he never

would have known how if, on waking somewhat
suddenly the last time she came, he had not seen
her leaning over him and gently withdrawing her
hands.

At first he thought it was an apparition and
shut his eyes that he might not see it; but having
subsequently asked his mother if Fanchon had felt
his head and pulse, or if he had dreamed, Mother
Barbeau, to whom her husband had at last disclosed something of his projects, and who desired
to see Sylvinet cured of his dislike to this young
girl, replied that she had indeed come three days
successively, both in the morning and evening,
and that she had marvellously cut short his fever
by secret means.   Sylvinet would not believe
this; he said his fever had gone of itself, and that
the words and secrets of Fanchon were vain and
foolish.   However, as he remained tranquil and
well for some days, Barbeau thought he ought to
profit by this occasion to announce to him the
possibility of his brother's marriage, without at
once naming the person he had in view.

"You have no need to conceal from me the
name of the future wife you destine for Landry,"
replied Sylvinet; "I know well it is this Fanchon,
who has succeeded in charming you all."

In truth, the result of Barbeau's secret inquiry
had been so favorable to Fanchon that, his doubts
being all removed, he greatly desired to recall
Landry.   His only fears now were for the jealousy of Sylvinet, and he tried to cure him of this
tendency by telling him that his brother would

never be happy without Fanchon; to which Sylvinet replied:

"Let this marriage take place, then, for my
brother must be happy."

But they dared not let it take place yet, for Sylvinet was again attacked with fever as soon as he
had given his consent.

CHAPTER XXIII.

BARBEAU feared lest Fanchon might preserve
a remembrance of his former injustice, and, that
being consoled for the absence of Landry, she
might think of some other lover. When, therefore, she came to the Bessonniere to nurse Sylvinet, he tried to speak to her of Landry, but she
pretended not to hear him, and he found himself
greatly embarrassed.

At last one morning he determined to go and
find Fanchon.

"Fanchon Fadet," he said to her, "I have come
to ask you a question, to which I beg you will
reply in all honesty and truth. Before the decease of your grandmother, had you any idea of
the wealth she would leave you?"

"Yes, Farmer Barbeau," replied Fanchon, "I
had some idea, because I had often seen her reckoning gold and silver, and I never saw anything
go out of the house but halfpence; and also because she had often said to me when other young

people mocked at my rags: 'Never mind them, my little one; you will be richer than any of them, and the day will come when you can be dressed in silk from head to foot, if such be your pleasure.'"

"And then," returned Barbeau, "did you make the fact known to Landry? If so, may it not have been on account of your money that my son pretended to be in love with you?"

"As for that, Farmer Barbeau," replied Fanchon, "having always cherished the idea of being loved for my 'beaux yeux,' which is the only good that has never been denied me, I was not fool enough to tell Landry that my real charm lay in the eel-skin purse, though I might have done so with perfect safety, for Landry loved me so honestly and truly that he never gave himself the trouble to ask whether I were rich or poor."

"And since your grandmother's decease, my dear Fanchon," continued Barbeau, "can you give me your word that Landry has neither been informed by you nor any other of the true state of the case?"

"I can," said Fanchon. "As truly as I love God, you are, besides myself, the only person in the world who is acquainted with the fact."

"And do you think, Fanchon, that Landry has retained his love for you? Since the decease of your grandmother have you received any proof that he has not been unfaithful to you?"

"I have received the very best proof," said she, "for I confess to you that he came to see me three days after this death, and swore that he should die of grief if he did not have me for his wife."

"And you, Fanchon, what reply did you make?"

"That, Farmer Barbeau, I am not obliged to tell you; still, I will answer if it will make you happy. I replied that we had yet time to think of marriage, and that I should not willingly decide in favor of a young man who courted me against the wishes of his relations."

And as Fanchon said this with a proud and an unembarassed air, Barbeau was somewhat uneasy.

"I have not the right to question you, Fanchon Fadet," said he, "and I know not whether you intend to render my son happy or miserable for life; but I know that he loves you devotedly, and were I in your place, entertaining the same notions you do of being loved for yourself, I should reason thus: 'Landry Barbeau loved me when I wore rags, when every one else repulsed me, and when even his relations visited that love upon him as a great sin; he thought me handsome when every one else denied me even the hope of becoming so; he has loved me in spite of the troubles this love has brought upon him; he has loved me absent or present—in short, he has loved me so well that I cannot distrust him, and will never think of any other for a husband.'"

"I have thought all this for a long time past, Farmer Barbeau," replied Fanchon; "but, I repeat it, I have the greatest repugnance to enter-

ing a family which is ashamed of me, and which
only consents to receive me from weakness and
compassion."

"If that be all which stands in the way, decide
at once, Fanchon," returned Barbeau; "for Landry's family bears you esteem, and desires to wel-
come you into it.   Do not think this change has
taken place because you are rich; it was not your
poverty which displeased us, but the bad reports
in circulation concerning you.   Had they been
well founded, my Landry might have died before
I would have consented to call you daughter-in-
law.   But I was determined to find the truth of
all these things.   I went to Chateau-Meillant on
purpose; I made the most minute inquiries there
and in our own neighborhood; and now I am satisfied that those reports were false, and that you
are a wise and honest girl, as Landry affirmed
with such warmth.   Therefore, Fanchon Fadet,
I have come to ask you to marry my son; and if
you say yes, he shall be here in eight days."

This overture, which she had clearly foreseen,
rendered Fanchon very happy; but, not desiring
to let this appear, since she wished to retain the
respect of the family she was about to enter, she
replied discreetly; whereupon Barbeau observed:

"I see, my child, some feeling still exists in
your heart against me and mine.   Do not require a man of my age to make you excuses; be
satisfied with an honest word; and when I tell
you that you will be loved and esteemed in our
house, you may trust to Farmer Barbeau, who

never yet deceived any one. Come, will you give
a kiss of peace to the guardian you have chosen,
or to the father who desires to adopt you?"

Fanchon could no longer hold out; she threw
both arms around the neck of Farmer Barbeau,
and his old heart was rejoiced.

Their arrangements were soon made. The
marriage was to take place at the expiration of
Fanchon's mourning. It only remained to recall Landry. But, when Mother Barbeau came
the same evening to see Fanchon, to embrace and
give her her blessing, she told her that at the news
of the approaching mariage of his brother Sylvinet had been taken ill again; and she begged
them to wait yet a few days, that he might be
cured or consoled.

"You committed an error, Mother Barbeau,"
said Fanchon, "in assuring Sylvinet that he did
not dream he saw me by his side as the fever left
him. Now his every thought is in opposition to
mine, and I have no longer the same power to
cure him as he sleeps. He may even repulse me,
and my presence may increase the mischief."

"I do not think so," replied Mother Barbeau,
"for just now, feeling ill, he went to bed, saying:
'Where, then, is this Fanchon? I believe she relieved me once; is she coming no more?' And I
told him I would fetch you, upon which he appeared contented and almost impatient."

"I will go," returned Fanchon; "only this time
I must take other means; for, I tell you, that what

succeeded when he did not know I was present
will no longer take effect."

"And will you take no drugs or remedies?" said
Mother Barbeau.

"No," replied Fanchon; "there is not much the
matter with his body; it is his mind with which
I have to deal, and I am going to try and invigor-
ate it by the influence of mine; but I do not insure
my success. The best I can promise is to wait
patiently for the return of Landry, and not to ask
you to send for him until we have done all we can
to restore his brother to health. Landry recommended him so strongly to my care that I know
he will approve of my retarding his return and
happiness."

When Sylvinet saw Fanchon by his bedside he
appeared dissatisfied, and would not tell her how
he felt. She wished to feel his pulse. but he drew
back his hand and turned his face to the wall.
Then Fanchon made signs to be left alone with
him; and when every one had gone out she extinguished the lamp, and only allowed the light of
the moon, which was at its full, to enter the chamber. She then returned to Sylvinet's side and
said, in a tone of authority, which he obeyed like
a child:

"Sylvinet, give both your hands into mine, and
answer me truly, for I am not taking all this trouble for money, and if I have come to nurse you, it
is not to be badly received and treated by you. Pay
attention, therefore, to what I am about to ask,

and to what you reply, for it will be impossible to deceive me."

"Ask me what you think fit, Fanchon," replied the twin, astonished to hear himself spoken to so severely by the little, laughing Fanchon, to whom, in times past, he had so often replied by throwing a stone.

"Sylvain Barbeau," she continued, "it appears you desire to die!"

Sylvinet hesitated a moment before he replied, but as Fanchon pressed his hand strongly, making him sensible of her will, he said, with much confusion:

"Would not death be the happiest thing that could come to me, since I know that I bring trouble upon my family by my bad health, and by"—

"Say on, Sylvain; you must conceal nothing from me."

"And by my gloomy mind, which I cannot change?" replied the twin, perfectly overcome.

"And also by your bad heart," said Fanchon, in a tone so harsh that his anger and fear were increased.

"Why do you accuse me of having a bad heart?" said he. "You say insulting things to me when you see I have not the strength to defend myself."

"I tell you truths, Sylvain," replied Fanchon; "and I am going to tell you more. I have no pity for your illness, because I know enough to see that it is not serious, and that if you are in any danger at all it is of becoming mad, to which end you do your best, unknowing whither your malice and weakness of mind lead you."

"Reproach me with weakness of mind, if you will," said Sylvinet; "but as for malice, it is a reproach I do not believe I deserve."

"Do not try to defend yourself," replied Fanchon; "I know you a little better than you know yourself, Sylvain, and I tell you weakness engenders falsehood; and this is why you are egotistical and ungrateful."

"If you think so ill of me, Fanchon Fadet, it must be because my brother Landry has greatly misrepresented me, and has thus shown you the little affection he bears me; for if you know, or think you know me, it can only be through him."

"This is just what I expected, Sylvain; I knew you would not utter three words without complaints and accusations against your twin; for the affection you entertain for him, in its foolish and ungovernable nature, verges on anger and spite. By this I know you are half mad, and not at all good. Well, now, I tell you, Landry loves you ten thousand times better than you love him, the proof of which is that he never reproaches you, make him suffer as you will, while you reproach him in all things, though he does nothing but yield and serve you. How could I fail to see the difference between you and him? Thus, the more good Landry has told me of you, the worse I have thought of you, because I consider that so good a brother cannot be misjudged but by an unjust soul."

"Then you hate me, Fanchon! I was not deceived on that point, at all events, and I knew you would deprive me of my brother's love by speaking ill of me."

"I expected this also, Master Sylvain, and I am glad you at last include me in the list of those who wrong you. I am going to reply by telling you that you have a bad heart, and that you are a child of falsehood, since you misjudge and insult a person who has always served and defended you, though knowing all the time you were opposed to her—a person who has a hundred times over deprived herself of the greatest, the only pleasure she had in the world, the pleasure of seeing Landry and remaining with him, to send Landry to you, and to give you the happiness of which she deprived herself. And yet I owed you nothing. You have always been my enemy, and as far back as I can remember I never met a child so harsh and haughty as you have ever been towards me. I might well have desired vengeance, and the opportunity has not been wanting. If I have not availed myself of it, and if, unknown to you, I have rendered you good for evil, it is because I have a great idea of what a Christian ought to forgive for the love of God. But when I speak to you of God, doubtless you do not understand me, for you are His enemy and the enemy of your own salvation."

"I have allowed you to say many things, Fanchon, but this is too much; you accuse me of being a heathen!"

"Have you not just told me you desired death? and do you believe this to be the thought of a Christian?"

"I did not say that, Fanchon; I said"——

And Sylvinet paused, frightened to think what he had said, as it appeared impious after the remonstrances of Fanchon.

But she did not leave him in peace, and continued to reprimand him:

"It may be," said she, "that your words are worse than your thoughts; for I often think you do not desire death, as it pleases you to make people believe, so that you may remain master in your family, to torment your mother, who is in despair about you, and your twin, who is simple enough to believe that you would indeed put an end to your days; but I am not your dupe, Sylvain; I believe you fear death as much, perhaps even more, than others, and that you are amused at the terror with which you inspire those who love you.   It pleases you to see the wisest and the most necessary measures yield to your threat of killing yourself; and, indeed, it is very convenient and pleasant only to have to speak a word to make those about one yield.   By this means you are the master of all here.   But, as it is against nature, and you have arrived at it by measures which God does not approve, God punishes you by rendering you still more miserable than you would be in obeying instead of commanding.   Thus you are weary of a life which is only too easy and idle.   I will tell you what you

wanted to make you a good and sensible boy—
you wanted harsh parents, great poverty, not always enough bread, and frequent blows.   Had
you been brought up in the same school as myself
and my brother Jeanot, instead of being so ungrateful, you would be thankful for the least
thing. Stay, Sylvinet, do not fall back upon your
twinship. I know a great deal too much has been
said in your hearing about this twin-love being a
law of nature, which must cause your death if opposed, and you have believed that you were only
obeying your fate by carrying this affection to
excess; but God is not so unjust as to doom any
of us to a bad fate before we are born.   He is not
so wicked as to give us thoughts which we cannot overcome; and you wrong Him, like a superstitious fool as you are, by believing that there is
in the blood of your body more power for evil
and misery than for virtue and happiness. Never,
unless you are indeed deranged, will I believe
that you cannot combat your jealousy if you
please.   But you will not, because this vice of
your soul has been too much caressed, and you
value your duty less than your fancy."

Sylvinet made no reply, but allowed Fanchon
to reprimand him for some time longer without
offering any excuse. He felt that she was right,
and that she only failed in indulgence on one
point; this was, that she appeared to think he had
never resisted his failing, but that he had in all
ways been selfish, without knowing or caring
that he was egotistical. This pained and humili-

13

ated him greatly, and he desired to inspire her with a better idea of him. As for Fanchon, she knew quite well that she exaggerated, and she did it on purpose to vex his mind before she undertook to soothe and console it. She forced herself, therefore, to speak harshly and to appear angry, while in her heart she felt such pity and affection for him that her dissimulation rendered her ill, and she left his side more weary and fatigued than her patient.

CHAPTER XXIV.

THE truth is, Sylvinet was not half so ill as he appeared, and as it pleased him to think. Fanchon, by feeling his pulse, had from the first recognized that the fever was not strong, and that, if he were somewhat delirious, it was because his mind was more enfeebled than his body. She endeavored, therefore, to obtain an influence over him by inspiring him with a great fear of herself, and at daylight returned to his side. He had scarcely slept, but he was tranquil, and, as it were, subdued. As soon as he saw her he held out his hand, instead of withdrawing it, as he had done the evening before.

"Why do you offer me your hand, Sylvain?" she said to him; "is it that I may see how your fever is? I can tell by your face it has left you."

Withdrawing his hand, which she would not

touch, Sylvinet said: "It was to bid you good morning, Fanchon, and to thank you for the trouble you take in my behalf."

"In that case I accept your good morning," said she, taking his hand and holding it in her own; "for I never refuse a frank offer, and do not think you sufficiently false to proffer a mark of interest if you do not feel it."

Sylvinet, though awake, experienced great comfort in holding his hand in that of Fanchon, and said to her, in a gentle voice:

"Nevertheless, you used me very ill yesterday evening, Fanchon, and I know not how it is I can overlook it; nay, even think you good to come and see me after all the reproaches you uttered."

Fanchon seated herself by his bed, and spoke very differently from the preceding evening. She now evinced such goodness, gentleness and tenderness that Sylvinet felt greatly soothed and pleased. He wept much, confessed all his wrongs, and even asked her pardon and her friendship so ingenuously that she quickly recognized his heart to be better than his head. She allowed him to give way to his feelings; still, at times, scolding him; but when she tried to withdraw her hand he retained it, feeling as though that hand cured both body and soul at the same time.

At length, finding him as she wished, she said:

"I will go now, Sylvain, and you must get up, for you have no longer any fever, and you must not lie in bed while your mother wearies herself with waiting upon you, and wastes her time by keeping you company. You will then eat what your mother will present you from me. It will be meat. I know you say you are disgusted with it, and that you will no longer live on anything but vegetables. But this is of no consequence. You must force your appetite, and, should you feel repugnance, you must not allow it to appear. It will give pleasure to your mother to see you eating solid food, and as for yourself, the repugnance, once surmounted and concealed, will be less strong the next time, and will cease to exist altogether the third. Try if I am deceiving you. Adieu, and do not cause me to be summoned again, for I know you will not be ill unless you desire to be so."

"You will not return, then, this evening?" said Sylvinet. "I should have thought you would come and see me again."

"I am not a paid doctor, Sylvinet, and I have other things to do than to take care of you when you are not ill."

"You are right, Fanchon; but the desire I have to see you—perhaps you think that, too, is egotism? But it is not so; it comforts me to talk to you."

"Well, you are not lame, and you know where I live. You know that I am to be your sister by marriage, as I already am by affection; you can therefore come and talk to me without any fear of blame."

"I will come, since you are willing," said Sylvinet. "I will get up now, Fanchon, though I have a bad headache, from want of sleep, and my misery during the night."

She laid her hand upon his forehead, and in five minutes he found himself so refreshed and consoled that he no longer felt as though anything was the matter with him.

"I see I was wrong to refuse your assistance, Fanchon, for you are very learned and know how to charm away sickness. All the other doctors did me mischief with their drugs; while you, by only touching me, have cured me. I think if I could be always near you you would prevent me from ever being sick and naughty. But tell me, Fanchon, are you no longer angry with me? and will you rely upon the pledge I have given you to submit myself to you entirely?"

"I do rely upon it," said she, "and unless you change your ideas I shall love you as though you were my twin. Come, Sylvain, get up, eat, talk, walk and sleep," she continued, rising; "this is my command for to-day. To-morrow you shall work."

"And I shall come and see you."

"So be it," said she.

And she departed with a look of affection and forgiveness, which suddenly gave him the strength and the desire to quit his bed of misery and idleness.

Mother Barbeau could not wonder enough at the skill of Fanchon, and in the evening she said to her husband

"Sylvinet is better than he has been for the last

six months. He has eaten everything I have
given him to-day, without his accustomed grim-
aces; and what is more astonishing still, he speaks
of Fanchon as though she were an angel. There
are no bounds to the good he attributes to her, and
he desires greatly the return and marriage of his
brother. It is like a miracle, and I know not
whether I am waking or sleeping."

"Miracle or no," said Barbeau, "that girl is
very wise, and I believe she must bring good luck
to a family."

Sylvinet departed three days after to seek his
brother at Arthon. He had asked his father and
Fanchon, as a great reward, to let him be the first
to announce to him his happiness."

"All my happiness comes upon me at once,"
said Landry, almost fainting in his brother's arms
with joy, "since it is you who have come to seek
me, and you appear as contented as myself."

They returned together without loitering by
the way, as may well be imagined; and there were
no happier people in the world than the people of
Bessonniere when they were all gathered around
the supper table, with Fanchon and the Grasshopper in the middle.

For half a year their lives flowed happily and
peacefully along. The young Nanette was be-
trothed to Cadet Caillaud, who, after his own
family, was the best friend Landry had. It was
settled that the two nuptials should take place at
the same time. Sylvinet had formed so great an
affection for Fanchon that he did nothing with-

out consulting her, and she had such perfect control over him that he seemed to look upon her as his mother, rather than his sister. He was no longer ill, and jealousy was quite out of the question. If at times he still appeared sad, Fanchon scolded him, and immediately he became smiling and communicative. The two marriages took place on the same day, and as the means were not wanting the wedding fete was so gay that Caillaud, who never in the whole course of his life before had committed the slightest excess, now actually appeared somewhat elated on the third day. Nothing interrupted the joy of Landry and the whole family, or it might be said of the entire country; for the two families, who were rich, and Fanchon, who was as rich as the Barbeaus and Caillauds put together, entertained every one with hospitality, and dispensed munificent charities. Fanchon's heart was too noble not to desire to render good for evil to all who had wronged her.

Subsequently, when Landry had bought a fine farm, which, through his own and his wife's knowledge, he managed admirably, she built a pretty house for the reception of the unfortunate children of the commune, and during four hours of every day in the week herself took the trouble, with the assistance of her brother Jeanot, to instruct them, teaching them true religion, and, moreover, assisting the most necessitous among them. She remembered how she herself was a poor forsaken child, and the children she brought into the world were taught at an early age to be kind and compassionate towards those who were neither so rich nor so beloved as themselves.

But what became of Sylvinet in the midst of all the happiness of his family? Why, something occurred to him which no one could comprehend, and which gave Barbeau much food for thought. About a month after the marriage of his brother and sister, as his father was urging him also to take a wife, he replied that he felt no disposition towards marriage, but that he had for some time entertained a wish which he should like to gratify, and that was to enter the army.

As the males of families in our parts are not too numerous, and the earth has no more arms to till it than it needs, a voluntary enlistment is seldom heard of. Thus every one was greatly astonished at this sudden resolution, for which Sylvinet could give no other reason than his fancy, and a military taste, which no one had ever suspected in him before. All that his father and mother, brothers and sisters, and Landry himself, could say, had no power to turn him from his purpose, and they were obliged to appeal to Fanchon, who was the adviser of the whole family.

She talked for two long hours with Sylvinet, and when they parted he had been weeping as well as his sister-in-law, and the manner of both was so tranquil and firm that no further objections could be offered when Sylvinet announced his determination to enlist, and Fanchon, approving his resolution, augured for him great good in the future. As no one could be sure that there was not more in all this than appeared, they dared no longer resist, and Mother Barbeau herself yielded, though not without shedding many tears. Landry was in despair, but his wife said to him:

"It is the will of God, and the duty of us all to allow Sylvinet to depart. Believe that I know well what I tell you, but you must never ask me to say more."

Landry accompanied his brother as far as he could, and as he restored him his bundle, which he had carried on his shoulder till the last moment, he felt as though he were giving his heart with it. Landry then returned to his beloved wife, who, for a long month had to nurse him through an illness brought on by grief.

As for Sylvain, he continued his route to the frontier, for it was the time of the great and glorious wars of the Emperor Napoleon. And, though he had never felt the slightest taste for a military life he conducted himself so well that he was soon renowned as a good soldier, brave in battle as a man who seeks only an opportunity for death, and yet gentle and submissive to discipline as a child; at the same time he was hardy in frame as the oldest veteran. As he had received sufficient education for advancement, it came quickly, and after ten years of fatigue, courage and good conduct, he was made a captain, with a cross of honor into the bargain.

"Ah, if he would but return!" said Mother Barbeau to her husband the evening of the day on which they had received from him a letter, full of affection for themselves and for Landry, for Fanchon, and, in short, for old and young of the family. "Here he is almost a general, and it is quite time for him to rest."

"The rank he has is sufficient," said Barbeau, "and is, at least, a great honor for a family of peasants!"

"This Fanchon foretold well what would happen," continued Mother Barbeau. "Yes, it has come to pass as she said!"

"I can never understand," said the farmer, "why Sylvinet's thoughts turned so suddenly in that direction, and how such a change came over his humor; he who was so quiet, so great a lover of his ease."

"My old man," said Mother Barbeau, "our daughter-in-law knows more of this than she is willing to tell; but a mother is not to be deceived, and I believe I know as much in this matter as our Fanchon.

"It is time then to tell me!" returned Barbeau.

"Well," replied his wife, "our Fanchon, you see, is a great charmer, and she charmed Sylvinet more than she desired. When she saw the charm working so strongly she would willingly have withdrawn or destroyed it, but she could not, and our Sylvinet, finding that he thought too much of his brother's wife, departed from a feeling of

honor and virtue, in which Fanchon sustained
and encouraged him."

"If it be so, indeed," said Barbeau, "I am
afraid he will never marry, for the bath-woman
of Clavieres said, in days gone by, that when once
Sylvinet fell in love with a woman he would no
longer be so infatuated with his brother, and
that, possessing a heart so sensitive and impas-
sioned, his first love would be his last."